THE PECULIAR CASE OF LORD FINSBURY'S DIAMONDS

THE CASEBOOK OF BARNABY ADAIR: VOLUME 2

STEPHANIE LAURENS

THE PECULIAR CASE OF LORD FINSBURY'S DIAMONDS

THE CASEBOOK OF BARNABY ADAIR: VOLUME 2

A tale of murder, mystery, passion, and intrigue—and diamonds!

Penelope Adair, wife and partner of amateur sleuth Barnaby Adair, is so hugely pregnant she cannot even waddle. When Barnaby is summoned to assist Inspector Stokes of Scotland Yard in investigating the violent murder of a gentleman at a house party, Penelope, frustrated that she cannot participate, insists that she and Griselda, Stokes's wife, be duly informed of their husbands' discoveries.

Yet what Barnaby and Stokes uncover only leads to more questions. The murdered gentleman had been thrown out of the house party days before, so why had he come back? And how and why did he come to have the fabulous Finsbury diamond necklace in his pocket, much to Lord Finsbury's consternation. Most peculiar of all, why had the murderer left the necklace, worth a stupendous fortune, on the body?

The conundrums compound as our intrepid investigators attempt to make sense of this baffling case. Meanwhile, the threat of scandal grows ever more tangible for all those attending the house party – and the stakes are highest for Lord Finsbury's daughter and the gentleman who has spent the last decade resurrecting his family fortune so he can aspire to her hand. Working parallel to Barnaby and Stokes, the would-be lovers hunt for a path through the maze of contradictory facts to expose the murderer, disperse the pall of scandal, and claim the love and the shared life they crave.

A pre-Victorian mystery with strong elements of romance. A short novel of 39,000 words.

PRAISE OF THE WORKS OF STEPHANIE LAURENS

"Stephanie Laurens' heroines are marvelous tributes to Georgette Heyer: feisty and strong." *Cathy Kelly*

"Stephanie Laurens never fails to entertain and charm her readers with vibrant plots, snappy dialogue, and unforgettable characters." *Historical Romance Reviews*

"Stephanie Laurens plays into readers' fantasies like a master and claims their hearts time and again." *Romantic Times Magazine*

OTHER TITLES BY STEPHANIE LAURENS

A Fine Passion

To Distraction

Beyond Seduction

The Edge of Desire

Mastered by Love

Black Cobra Quartet

The Untamed Bride

The Elusive Bride

The Brazen Bride

The Reckless Bride

The Adventurers Quartet

The Lady's Command

A Buccaneer at Heart

The Daredevil Snared

Lord of the Privateers

The Cavanaughs

The Designs of Lord Randolph Cavanaugh (April 24, 2018)

Other Novels

The Lady Risks All

The Legend of Nimway Hall – 1750: Jacqueline

Medieval (As M.S. Laurens)

Desire's Prize

THE PECULIAR CASE OF
LORD FINSBURY'S
DIAMONDS

THE PECULIAR CASE OF LORD FINSBURY'S DIAMONDS

Copyright © 2014 by Savdek Management Proprietary Limited

ISBN: 978-0-9922789-3-9

Cover design by Savdek Management Pty. Ltd.

Savdek Management Proprietary Limited, Melbourne, Australia.

www.stephanielaurens.com

Email: admin@stephanielaurens.com

The name Stephanie Laurens is a registered trademark of Savdek Management Proprietary Ltd.

❀ Created with Vellum

CHAPTER 1

DECEMBER 1836, LONDON

*T*he front doorbell of Number 24 Albemarle Street pealed.

The chiming was immediately followed by a peremptory knock.

Penelope Adair, lady of the house, hugely pregnant and lying on the sofa in her garden parlor feeling like nothing so much as a beached whale, turned her head and peered through her spectacles at the clock on the mantelpiece.

She hadn't dozed off—it truly was barely nine o'clock.

Only one sort of summons appeared at their door at such an unfashionably early hour.

"Damn!" With effort, she pushed herself up into a semi-sitting position and jammed a cushion behind her aching back. She squinted down at the mound distending her belly. "You realize what this means? Stokes needs our help with a case, but I have to remain here, because with you in there I can barely waddle, much less investigate. The list of entertainments I'm giving up on your account is about to grow longer."

Over the last two weeks, she'd taken to addressing her imminent offspring, deeming it appropriate for them to grow accustomed to her voice. Another week or so...assuming she survived; the burden was getting exceedingly...burdensome.

Straining her ears, she heard Mostyn, their majordomo, cross the tiles of the front hall. The front door opened; after a minute punctuated by the rumble of male voices, Penelope heard the door close.

The rumble of voices continued; two voices, both recognizable. Penelope's husband, Barnaby Adair, third son of the Earl of Cothelstone and occasional consultant to the Metropolitan Police, had, it seemed, been equally quick in recognizing the import of the unexpected caller; he'd come out of the library in which, over the last week or so, he'd taken to lurking to intercept Mostyn and whatever message had been delivered.

Penelope leaned back against her supporting cushions. She was perfectly aware that, given the choice, Barnaby would much rather have lurked in the garden parlor, hovering within sight of her, but he'd wisely realized that that might be one protective step too far.

So he dallied in the library within easy reach—within hearing if she screamed.

Penelope sighed. "I wonder what sort of juicy case Stokes has for—" She broke off, then, jaw firming, went on, "For *us*." She glanced at her belly. "Just because I'm stuck here incubating you, and even though my mind sometimes wanders ridiculously, that doesn't mean that I can't, if I wish, concentrate enough to analyze facts."

The door opened. Barnaby walked in, a note in his hand. Meeting her gaze, he closed the door. Crossing the room, he drew one of the armchairs closer, then sat and leaned forward, his forearms on his thighs, so that his face was level with hers. He searched her eyes. "How are you feeling?"

She arched a brow. "An hour bigger and heavier than I felt over breakfast."

He didn't know what to say to that—what was safe to say to that.

She nodded at the note. "Stokes?"

Barnaby glanced at the short note. "Yes." He felt torn. He and Stokes —Inspector Basil Stokes of Scotland Yard, now a good friend alongside whom Barnaby frequently worked—had hoped that over the last weeks of Penelope's pregnancy the ton would take a brief holiday from crime, but, sadly, the ton hadn't obliged. "Stokes has been called to a murder at Finsbury Court, Lord Finsbury's house near Hampstead. A gentleman house guest was found bashed to death on a path near the house. Stokes writes that while he has yet to interview Lord Finsbury, from the reactions of the butler and the local constable it's clear he's going to need my assistance to be able to investigate."

Looking up, Barnaby saw Penelope grimace, but he couldn't tell if that was due to the baby or the situation.

It proved to be the latter. Rather grumpily, she admitted, "I know

Stokes wouldn't send for you, not at the moment, unless he genuinely needs your help."

That was undeniably true; with Stokes's wife, Griselda, also pregnant, albeit a few months less so than Penelope, Stokes was highly sympathetic to the emotional pressure Barnaby was experiencing.

He hesitated, then asked, "So should I go, or would you rather I remained here?"

"You should go." Shifting restlessly, Penelope pulled a face at him. "I'm only annoyed because I can't go with you—which leads to my one condition."

Rising, he arched his brows. "Which is?"

"That when you come home, you tell me *all*—no censoring of the facts to spare my delicate sensibilities, which, I assure you, pregnancy hasn't changed in the least. If anything I'm *less* delicate than I was before —being an almost-mother makes one rather bloody-minded over any sort of threat—so I want to know every last little detail."

So she could analyze. And he would be the first to admit that with her highly logical brain, she was exceptionally good at fathoming criminals' motives and intentions. It was what had first brought them together, and was one of the many things about her that continued to intrigue him.

Looking down at her face, he let his gaze drink in her delicate features, the aristocratically imperious tilt of her chin, and the dark depths of her deep brown eyes. Despite the drain of these latter weeks of pregnancy, the resolution and determination that were an integral part of her still shone clearly. She continued to fascinate him; she would always hold his heart.

He smiled, nodded. "Agreed." Leaning down, he brushed his lips over hers, lingered for two heartbeats, savoring the instant, compulsive connection, then he drew back and met her eyes. "And in return, no trying to go for a walk alone. Be good while I'm gone."

Penelope snorted. "Mama will be arriving within the hour—I won't have any choice."

As she'd intended, the reminder that her mother would be there to keep her company through the long, wearying day eased some of Barnaby's lingering concern, yet still he hesitated, his gaze on her. Feigning a pout, she waved dismissively. "Go, go—before I change my mind."

He laughed and turned to the door.

Settling back on her cushions, she called, "Just remember to take especial note of all the things I'll want to know."

Smiling, he glanced back and saluted her, then he left.

When the door closed behind him, Penelope sighed. After a moment, she glanced at her belly. "Told you. I'm missing out on investigating a murder..." She paused; gaze rising, she stared into space. Then, tilting her head, she patted her balloon-like belly. "But just analyzing the facts, having only them to work from, is undoubtedly a different sort of challenge."

After a moment, she reached for the large hand-bell Mostyn had left on the side table and rang it. When he answered, she asked him to fetch her traveling writing desk.

She spent the next fifteen minutes penning a note to Griselda Stokes. Penelope and Griselda had met during the investigation that had brought Penelope and Barnaby, and Stokes and Griselda, together; the two women were now firm friends, long past the need to stand on any ceremony, much less observe the strictures of social class, something Penelope rarely felt bound by regardless. In her note, she included what little she knew of Stokes's new case and that he had summoned Barnaby to assist him. She concluded with an invitation to Griselda and Stokes to join Penelope and Barnaby for dinner in Albemarle Street—although also pregnant, Griselda could still leave her house—so they could all share the latest findings and discuss what their husbands had thus far learned. Penelope ended her missive with the statement that she and Griselda being heavy with child didn't mean that they couldn't contribute.

Simply writing the words left her feeling more engaged.

After dispatching the letter via Mostyn, Penelope sat back and considered her mood—unexpectedly satisfied with her morning and excitedly expectant in looking forward to her evening, and, indeed, the days to come.

Murders were rarely solved in one day.

A sharp kick to her insides made her wince and refocus on her belly. Stroking one hand soothingly over the taut mound, she said, "You know, it's really very much better out here. You could kick to your heart's content. Feel free to join us at any time."

As the child quieted, Penelope's mind shifted to Stokes's new case. "I must remember to ask Mama what she knows about Lord Finsbury."

❧

Surrounded by old, tall trees, the spaces between filled with thick bushes,

Inspector Basil Stokes stood on a woodland path high on the shoulder of Haverstock Hill and looked down at the body of a man—a gentleman by his tailoring—that lay sprawled stomach-down on the grassy ground. The man's head and shoulders were twisted about as if he'd been looking up and back, but, courtesy of the damage wrought by a heavy implement, little remained of his features. Without inflection, Stokes asked, "What do you think?"

Standing beside Stokes, Barnaby surveyed the body. "Well, he's certainly dead."

The man had been of a good height, perhaps a touch over six feet tall, built lean and well-muscled, with dark wavy hair, fashionably cut. His clothes had been tailored, but not in Savile Row, and his linens appeared to be of decent quality. In lieu of any clear features—none were discernible in what remained of the man's face—his hands were the best indicator; studying the long fingers, the neatly manicured nails, Barnaby grimaced. "And you're right—he was a gentleman."

Barnaby had driven himself out of London in his curricle. Hampstead village, which lay at the far end of the path, was a coaching halt on the top of Haverstock Hill. Following Stokes's directions, it had taken Barnaby less than an hour to reach the coaching inn where Stokes had sent a constable to meet him—to lead him up this bucolic woodland path to the murder scene.

Gaze rising from the corpse, Barnaby looked in the direction in which the man appeared to have been walking. "How far on is Finsbury Court?"

Stokes grunted. "About a hundred yards before you walk onto the side lawn, but with all these trees and bushes, that's far enough away for no one there to have seen or heard anything."

Registering the disgusted note in Stokes's voice, Barnaby looked again at the body. Hiking up his trouser legs, he crouched to get a closer look at what was left of the man's face. "So he, whoever he is, walks up from the village, heading for Finsbury Court…this path leads nowhere else?"

Stokes glanced at the young constable who was standing rather stiffly at ease to one side. "Duffet?"

"No, sir." Duffet swallowed rather nervously. "It's purely a short-cut between the village and the Court."

Nodding, Barnaby continued, "So our victim walks up the path—and steps into a foot-trap." Looking down the body to where the steel jaws of a trap had clamped unforgivingly around the man's right ankle, Barnaby winced. Shifting, he looked more closely at the trap, which had been concealed in a natural dip in the ground, and confirmed that the contraption was well-anchored via the usual steel pegs. "I think we can assume that the trap immobilized him. That said, if he'd had time to come to grips with the pain, he would probably have been able to release himself— except that whoever set the trap was waiting, and as soon as our man was on the ground, they stepped in and bashed his skull in with..." Barnaby glanced up inquiringly.

The young constable had fine, gingery hair. Looking even paler than before, he held up a long-handled sledgehammer. "We found this slung into the bushes over there." With his head, he indicated a thick clump several yards closer to the house.

Barnaby frowned. "Was it just flung there, or had there been some attempt made to hide it?"

"Just flung, sir. We—the butler and me—saw the handle sticking out when we came down the path. The butler, Riggs, said as he thinks it's the hoop-hammer from the croquet shed. Apparently old Miss Finsbury— she's his lordship's sister—wanted a long-handled one so she could thump in the hoops without having to bend down."

"I see." Frowning, Barnaby rose. He glanced at Stokes. "In your note, you said the victim was a house guest. Do we know who he is?"

"A Mr. Peter Mitchell." Stokes consulted his notebook. "And although he *was* a guest at the house party still underway at Finsbury Court, it seems he was shown the door three days ago."

Barnaby met Stokes's eyes. "Any notion as to why?"

"Apparently," Stokes dryly returned, "we'll need to address such inquiries to his lordship in person."

Barnaby arched his brows but made no comment.

Stokes went on, "Mitchell left the house, bags and all, and was driven to the coaching inn—the same one you stopped at—late in the afternoon three days ago. Duffet asked, and the inn folk say Mitchell purchased a ticket and managed to squeeze onto the London coach that afternoon, and rattled off to town. No one at the house saw anything more of him until this morning, when the cook sent the scullery maid to fetch more eggs from a nearby farm, and the maid took the path and found him"—Stokes nodded at the body—"like this. Unsurprisingly, the maid went into hysterics, rushed back to the house, and alerted the staff. The butler sent for Duffet here, who came, saw, and sent word to the Yard."

"So," Barnaby said, "thus far only we three, and the butler and the scullery maid, have seen the body."

"And the murderer," Stokes grimly replied.

"Indeed." Barnaby glanced at Duffet, then looked back at Stokes. "Any clue as to when it was done? From the relative dryness beneath the body versus the dampness on his back, I would assume it was sometime yesterday."

Stokes nodded. "According to the butler, Mitchell had sent word two evenings ago that he would be returning to speak with Miss Finsbury yesterday afternoon. He was expected, but he never appeared. Duffet checked, and Mitchell did arrive on the coach that stopped at Hampstead yesterday afternoon."

"So the murderer knew Mitchell was coming to the house and guessed he would be walking up this path. The murderer seized the chance and set the trap, and kept watch. When Mitchell stepped into the trap and went down, the murderer emerged from the bushes and repeatedly struck him until he was most assuredly dead. Then the murderer flung the hoop-hammer into the bushes and..." Frowning, Barnaby paused.

"Walked back to the house," Stokes filled in. "That's the most likely scenario. No one in the village saw any stranger around yesterday afternoon, arriving or leaving, other than Mitchell himself."

Stokes paused, then went on, "But that's not the end of the complications."

When Barnaby looked his way, Stokes said, "On being shown the body, Duffet searched Mitchell's pockets—and found a diamond necklace."

Barnaby glanced at Duffet.

The young man's face lit. "A fabulous thing, sir. It glittered like stars."

"According to the butler, who, Duffet says, goggled as much as he did, the necklace belongs to Lord Finsbury." Stokes read from his notebook. "It's known as the Finsbury diamonds, is hugely valuable, and, in some circles at least, is well-known."

Barnaby grimaced. "Old family jewelry, unless stolen, holds little interest for me, but if we need to know more, I know who to ask."

"Cynster?" When Barnaby nodded, Stokes said, "It's possible we might need to know more about the necklace, but at this point I can think of several more urgent questions."

"But"—Barnaby glanced from Stokes to Duffet—"where are the diamonds now?"

"As mentioned," Stokes grimly said, "the butler, Riggs, went into a tizzy at the sight of them, and he insisted they be immediately returned to his master. Duffet here, not understanding the usual procedures of a murder investigation, allowed himself to be swayed. He and Riggs took the diamonds back to Lord Finsbury."

Eyes on Duffet, Barnaby asked, "How did Lord Finsbury react?"

Obviously regretting his unintentional lapse, Duffet hurried to assure him, "Exactly as one might expect, sir. He was stunned and shocked."

"Apparently," Stokes said, "Lord Finsbury had no idea the diamonds weren't in the safe in his study."

"He really was rattled, sir," Duffet opined. "Went pale as a sheet. Then he took the diamonds and put them back in the safe—in a black velvet box, which he said was where he'd thought they'd been."

Barnaby struggled to fit the puzzle piece of the diamonds into the picture of the murder forming in his mind. After several seconds, he met Stokes's gaze. "That's…a very confounding complication."

"Indeed." Stokes glanced at the body, then slid his notebook into his greatcoat pocket. "If you've seen all you need to see here, I suggest we go and speak with Lord Finsbury. The message I received, conveyed by the butler, was that his lordship is not best pleased to have the police about and he wants us out of his hair and off his property as soon as may be."

They covered the body with a canvas and weighed it down with rocks. "The police surgeon's men should be along any minute." Stokes glanced at Duffet. "You left directions for them at the inn?"

"One of the stable lads will show them the way." Duffet set the last rock in place.

With an approving nod, Stokes turned toward the house.

Starting up the path, pacing side by side, shoulder to shoulder with Stokes, with Duffet falling in behind, Barnaby quietly said, "Lord Finsbury can want and even demand all he likes, but this is murder—violent murder—and the guilty party has to be identified and brought to account."

Stokes's lips curled in a cynical little smile. "Which is why you're here."

Barnaby humphed. As they walked toward the house, while he mentally rehearsed the arguments with which to persuade Lord Finsbury of the unavoidable necessity of a detailed investigation, another part of his mind was busy juggling all the bits of evidence he'd already absorbed.

Reaching the end of the path, they stepped out of the screening trees and bushes onto a swath of lawn.

Barnaby and Stokes both halted, in wordless accord seizing the moment to study the house and glean all that the sight could tell them. A sprawling old manor with central parts dating from Tudor times, the building was larger than Barnaby had anticipated. A small forest of tall, ornate chimneys rose above the lead roof; it was the first week of December and smoke rose in thin columns from half a dozen terracotta pots. They were facing the southwest façade; the front entrance lay around the corner to their right, where the carriage drive emerged from the trees to end in a graveled forecourt. From where they stood they couldn't see the front door.

Roughly half of the house had two stories with attics above, while the rest was comprised of ground-floor rooms somewhat haphazardly attached to the original structure.

Stokes stirred; having looked his fill, he was ready to move on.

Holding his ground, Barnaby murmured, "The price for my presence was a promise that I would tell Penelope all."

From the corner of his eye, he saw Stokes's lips quirk in a wolfish—teasing but understanding—grin. "Ah—I see." Stokes settled again.

Barnaby consciously tried to see the house as Penelope—or, for that matter, Griselda—would; he and Stokes had learned that both ladies saw things neither he nor Stokes did. Or, rather, deduced relevance from details neither he nor Stokes even registered.

So he looked at the curtains, at how many rooms showed signs of occupation rather than being closed up. He noted the kempt-ness—the paintwork, how clean the windows were, the neatness of the flowerbeds. In the end, he simply tried to fix the picture in his mind.

Shifting, he glanced at Stokes. "I have no idea what we've missed, but I'm sure there'll be something."

Stokes grinned and they started walking across the lawn—a touch over-long—toward the front of the house.

When they rounded the corner and stepped onto the gravel of the fore-court, Barnaby halted again, taking another moment to fix an image of the front façade in his mind.

That done, he blinked, and his mind swung back to the body. To the question that kept niggling.

Stokes was patiently waiting. Meeting his eyes, Barnaby said, "If, unbeknown to Lord Finsbury, Mitchell had this fabulous necklace in his keeping, why was he bringing it back to Finsbury Court?"

Stokes held Barnaby's gaze, then nodded and looked at the house. "Let's go and find out."

Side by side, greatcoats swinging, they headed for the front steps.

In the shadows cast by the curtains of the bow window in the drawing room of Finsbury Court, Frederick Culver stood beside Gwendolyn Finsbury. Both studied the men who had paused in the forecourt to look up at the house before striding toward the front door.

"The first two don't look like policemen." Gwen slanted a glance at Frederick. "Do you think that's who they are?"

The men in question climbed the porch steps and moved out of Gwen and Frederick's sight; Duffet, the local constable, followed. Turning his head, Frederick met Gwen's gaze. "I don't know, but we were told to expect an inspector from London—the dark-haired one might be he. He looks grim enough. The other..." Frederick frowned. "I don't know about him—he doesn't fit the bill."

The second man, the one with curly fair hair, had moved with a certain indolent grace that in Frederick's experience usually signaled a member of the upper echelons of the ton. "Then again, appearances can be deceiving."

They certainly had been in Peter Mitchell's case.

Gwen didn't need to hear the words to know what Frederick was thinking; the tightening of his mobile lips was indication enough. And, truth be told, she was still somewhat stunned at Mitchell's transformation from charming gentleman to loutish libertine.

Turning from the now empty forecourt, she let her gaze travel the room, taking in all those seated on the sofas or in armchairs, or, in the case of Algernon Rattle, posing before the fireplace. Algernon was present because he was courting Miss Harriet Pace, daughter of Gwen's Aunt Agnes's old friends, Mr. Herbert Pace and Mrs. Olivia Pace. A close friend of Gwen's, Harriet presently sat beside her mother on the corner of the sofa closest to Algernon, with whom she was conducting a low-voiced conversation. Beside her, Mrs. Pace was chatting earnestly to Agnes, seated on the other end of the sofa, and Mrs. Lucy Shepherd, who, along with her daughter, Juliet, occupied a love-seat angled to that end of the sofa.

Also a friend of Gwen's, Juliet was pretending to listen to the older ladies, but Gwen would have wagered that Juliet was actually thinking—dreaming—of her fiancé, Mr. Jeremy Finch, who was a secretary in the Home Office and presently traveling with the Minister.

The older gentlemen, Mr. Pace and Mr. Thomas Shepherd, were quietly chatting in two armchairs on the other side of the room.

Everyone present had been invited by Agnes. The only exception had been Mr. Peter Mitchell, who had been invited by Gwen's father; as Gwen understood it, her father had decided to invite Mitchell and had subsequently asked Agnes to organize a house party, and, as usual, had left all the rest to Agnes.

That being so, Gwen had yet to comprehend the reason behind the frown her father had directed at Frederick when Frederick had arrived. Admittedly her father wouldn't have expected to see Frederick, who had only that week returned from countless years in deepest Africa. However, given that Frederick was the only child of the Culvers, longtime neighbors now deceased, who had been very close friends with her father, her late mother, and Agnes, who, as a spinster, had lived at Finsbury Court all her life, Gwen was at a loss to account for the antipathy she'd detected in her father's welcome. Aside from all else, Frederick was Agnes's godson.

It was Agnes who had run Finsbury Court ever since Gwen's mother had died over a decade ago. Gwen was very close to her aunt, who had never attempted to step into her mother's shoes with respect to Gwen herself, but, instead, had always been there, a rock-solid support.

What truly mystified Gwen was that the only instance she could recall of her father involving himself in any social decision was his invitation to Peter Mitchell—and look how that had turned out!

"Murder." She whispered the word. After a moment, she murmured, "Everyone is talking about inconsequential things, but, inside, all of us are wondering who murdered Peter Mitchell—and why."

Frederick arched a brow. "I think the overwhelming consideration goes somewhat deeper into self-interest than that." A cynical comment, but, he was certain, all too true.

Gwen looked at his face. Studied his expression. "What do you mean?"

Frederick met her gaze. "I mean that the primary question in the minds of everyone here who isn't the murderer goes more along the lines of: Will there be a scandal? And, if so, will it affect me?" He grimaced and added, "Or my daughter and her chances of a good marriage? Or my husband's connections? Or my wife's social standing?" He surveyed the group, then looked at Gwen. "You know as well as I how it goes."

She held his gaze for an instant, then nodded and looked again at the others. The potential for scandal, the possibility of being tainted by it, was, indeed, the threat hovering over them all.

The clang of the doorbell echoed through the house.

All conservations suspended. Everyone strained to hear…

Footsteps—Riggs's—crossing the front hall. The telltale squeak of the front door being opened.

Murmurs, but in deep voices too low to make out any words. Then the sound of the front door closing.

Everyone waited, breath bated.

Footsteps again, this time more than just Riggs's, but fading away, presumably down the corridor to Lord Finsbury's study where his lordship had retreated to await the arrival of the police.

Algernon eased out an audible breath and smiled winningly at Harriet, Mrs. Pace, and Agnes. "His lordship will take care of the authorities— just see if I'm not right. No need for us to be involved." He lifted an elegant shoulder. "None of us knew Mitchell, after all—no reason any of us would have wished him harm."

Algernon's gaze briefly rose to Frederick's face, then smoothly slid away as Mr. Pace and Mr. Shepherd both seconded Algernon's comforting reassurance.

Frederick glanced at Gwen. "I fear that's wishful thinking. Perhaps in the past such incidents could be brushed aside, but not these days." He wanted to warn her; ignoring what was likely to come wouldn't help her weather the storm.

She met his gaze, read his eyes, then nodded. "I suspect you're right."

He watched as she drew in a deeper breath; resolution, and a strength she hadn't had years ago, seeped into her expression and etched her fine features.

Features the memory of which had kept him going—struggling and working to the limit of his capacity—throughout his long years in Africa. He'd always loved Gwen, although he was certain she had never known. From the time she'd been an awkward ten-year-old tumbling out of trees —he'd laughed and caught her and admired her spirit. His fascination with her had started then.

And had matured with the years. He had never questioned it; the emotion had simply always been a part of him. Gwendolyn Finsbury had been created for him.

Then his parents had lost much of their wealth in a fraudulent investment scheme and he had had to do something. He'd been good with languages, good at managing people; he had signed on with a company eager to expand their mines in Africa.

He'd worked hard. He'd succeeded.

Then his parents had died and he'd realized that although he'd amassed a fortune, he had no assured future, no one with whom to share his life.

It had taken several months to arrange, but he had come back to England with his heart in his hands, hoping against hope that Gwen would still be there. Still unmarried, still the same fascinating girl. Agnes had written occasional letters, but he had never given his godmother any reason to suppose that he was in love with her niece.

And he had never, ever, done anything to communicate his feelings to Gwen.

Within a day of returning to his parents' house and sending a note around to Agnes, he'd received an invitation to the Finsbury Court house party. He'd deemed that beyond fortuitous, a sign that Fate had elected to smile on his suit and hand him the perfect situation in which to gauge Gwen's feelings toward him, and, if the signs were propitious, to make his feelings known to her and beg for her hand in marriage.

He'd arrived at Finsbury Court—and instead of the girl he remembered, a woman had smiled sweetly at him and given him her hand.

He'd been ridiculously tongue-tied, smitten all over again, but in a much more adult way.

The Gwen who stood beside him now was not the girl he'd idolized, who he had set on a pedestal and worshipped from afar.

She was so much more.

She had facets he hadn't imagined, layers he longed to explore.

And he wanted her with an even greater, more burning desire than before.

From that first instant, his attention had locked on her and hadn't wavered.

And she'd seemed to return his regard.

Then Mitchell had laid hands on her and—

Frederick drew in a deeper breath of his own and quietly stated, "In case it crosses your mind, I didn't even think of killing him—not even at the time."

Gwen's lips twisted. "I can honestly state that you're a better man than I." Briefly, she met his gaze. "I did think of it—for a fleeting moment. He made me so furious." She paused, then added, her voice lowering to a whisper, "I feared you might think that I'd encouraged him, perhaps to make you jealous—"

"No." Lips thinning, Frederick shook his head. "That didn't even occur to me." He glanced down and met her hazel eyes. A moment passed, then he simply said, "I know you."

And, he realized, he did.

CHAPTER 2

*B*arnaby followed Stokes through the door the butler, Riggs, held wide. Lord Finsbury's study was located down a corridor off the front hall; with Penelope's instructions high in his mind, Barnaby had used the moments since entering the house to look about him. Accustomed as he was to the homes of the ton's elite, the interior of Finsbury Court did not match his expectations; instead, the furnishings echoed the exterior—a bit of a hodgepodge, and while everything had once been of good quality, most items appeared worn, even a trifle shabby.

One quick, comprehensive glance informed him that his lordship's study was at one with the rest of the house.

Somewhat unexpectedly, Lord Finsbury was standing in the middle of the room in front of a large desk and the pair of chairs facing it, an unsubtle indication that he expected this meeting to be too short to warrant sitting down. Of average height and build, and showing a tendency to portliness, with thinning gray-brown hair, heavy brows nearly meeting over a patrician nose, and an expression of deep resistance, his lordship appeared a veritable caricature of an old-school peer of the stuffy, reactionary, stiff-upper-lip sort. Predictably, he frowned at Stokes as Stokes halted on the rug before him.

Stokes inclined his head. "Lord Finsbury. I'm Inspector Stokes of Scotland Yard."

Finsbury's gaze had already moved on to Barnaby.

"And," Stokes smoothly continued, "this gentleman is the Honorable

Barnaby Adair. The Chief Commissioner has requested that Mr. Adair assist in this case to ensure that the social ramifications are kept to a minimum."

That wasn't exactly the Chief Commissioner's direction, but Stokes and Barnaby had learned that those words best served to excuse Barnaby's presence and ease their way. Duly adopting a reassuring expression, Barnaby halted beside Stokes and nodded to Finsbury. "My lord. Rest assured the inspector and I will endeavor to conduct our investigation as expeditiously, and as discreetly, as possible. And with as little disruption to your house guests as we can manage."

Lord Finsbury's frown deepened until his shaggy brows formed a single line. "I really don't see that there can be any connection with anyone in this house. Mitchell was murdered in the woods—presumably by some vagabond."

Barnaby could almost hear Stokes's inward sigh.

"As to the matter of Mr. Mitchell's death, my lord"—Stokes's voice took on an authoritative edge—"I'm unsure how much you've heard, but the gentleman was first incapacitated by a foot-trap, then beaten to death with a hammer identified as the hoop-hammer from your croquet shed. It's clear the gentleman was headed for the house and he had, indeed, sent word that he would arrive yesterday afternoon. We also understand that, several days ago, an altercation of sorts occurred between the victim and other members of the house party resulting in the victim's ejection from the house. In short, my lord, all the evidence before us suggests that Mitchell was murdered by someone with, at the very least, access to this house and knowledge of recent happenings within it. Against that, we have thus far found no evidence of any stranger in the vicinity, vagabond or otherwise."

Lord Finsbury drew himself up and attempted to look down his nose at Stokes, who was several inches taller. "I find the suggestion that anyone presently in this house was involved in such a crime utterly preposterous."

"Be that as it may, my lord"—Barnaby's tones were more dulcet, yet held no more softness than Stokes's—"the law requires a full investigation of such cases and there is no avoiding that necessity."

Lord Finsbury stared at Barnaby for several moments, his pale blue gaze searching.

Barnaby looked back unmoving. Immovable.

Lord Finsbury glanced briefly at Stokes, then deflated. "Very well."

Lips thin, he peevishly gestured at the butler to leave them. Rounding his desk, he waved Barnaby and Stokes to the chairs facing it. "But I will hold you to your claim of discretion. And expeditiousness."

"It is our intention to settle this matter as soon as may be." Sitting, Stokes drew out his notebook; thus far, the interview had gone much as he'd expected. "If you could answer the questions we have to this point, it will assist us in keeping the disruption to your household to a minimum."

When his lordship said nothing, merely waited, tight-lipped, Stokes asked, "Who are the guests presently staying at Finsbury Court?"

Clasping his hands on the blotter, his lordship rattled off names—the Shepherds, the Paces, Algernon Rattle, and Frederick Culver.

"And your connection with these people?" Stokes asked.

Lord Finsbury paused, then offered, "The Shepherds and the Paces are friends of Agnes, my sister. I know them through her, although our acquaintance has stretched for many years. Their daughters, Juliet and Harriet, are friends of my daughter, Gwendolyn. As for Rattle, he's a younger man and I gather he's hanging about Harriet's skirts, but I know relatively little of him."

Stokes arched a brow. "And Culver?"

His features hardening, Lord Finsbury dipped his head. "I've known Frederick Culver all his life. His late parents were neighbors, but fell on hard times and Frederick left the country adventuring—I believe in Africa. He's Agnes's godson. It was she who invited him—I had no idea he would be here until he arrived."

Stokes tried to read Lord Finsbury's expression. "Am I to take it you don't approve of Culver?"

Lord Finsbury hesitated, then raised one shoulder. "I know little of the man he might now be, but he was the one who threw Mitchell out two— no, three—days ago. They nearly came to blows, I understand."

"Over what?" Barnaby asked.

"As to that, I wasn't there, so cannot say. You must inquire of those who were present."

"And they would be?" Barnaby prompted.

With obvious reluctance, Finsbury replied, "My daughter, Gwendolyn, and Culver. Agnes was involved as well, although to what extent I can't say."

Eyes on his notebook, Stokes nodded.

"The one guest you haven't mentioned is Mitchell himself." Barnaby caught Finsbury's gaze. "How did he come to be here?"

Stokes looked up and saw Finsbury's defensiveness intensify, but Finsbury worked to keep his tone level as he said, "I invited Mitchell. I met him at White's, and he seemed the right sort to introduce to Gwendolyn. She's twenty-three and I would like to see her appropriately settled."

Barnaby managed to stop himself from glancing at the shabby furnishings. "I take it Mitchell was wealthy?"

Lord Finsbury's lips pinched even more. "I had reason to believe he was well-off. He spoke of business successes in the colonies and the Americas."

Stokes was scribbling madly. "Do you know of any particular company? Any specific association?"

Finsbury frowned as if wracking his memories, but, eventually, he shook his head. "No—he never mentioned any name."

"Where in England did he hail from?" Barnaby asked.

Again, Finsbury shook his head. "It never came up. His accent was... well, he was one of us. Eton, Harrow, Winchester—something of that sort."

Or any good grammar school. Barnaby kept the words from his tongue and instead asked, "So your sister Agnes had organized a house party and you invited Mitchell to join you."

Finsbury's lips tightened. "No. I invited Mitchell, then I asked Agnes to arrange the house party to..."

"Provide social cover for introducing Mitchell to your daughter." Barnaby nodded easily. "Entirely understandable—that's how it's often done, after all."

At Barnaby's tone, Finsbury's bristling subsided somewhat.

"Now," Stokes said, "to the diamond necklace found in Mitchell's pocket." Stokes looked inquiringly at Finsbury. "I understand the necklace belongs to you."

"Yes." Finsbury's expression dissolved into one of transparently genuine confusion. "And before you ask, I have no idea how Mitchell came to have it in his possession. Until your constable showed it to me, I believed the necklace to be in its box in the wall safe behind that picture." Finsbury nodded to a portrait of some disapproving ancestor hanging on the wall to his right. "The box was still there, in its accustomed place, but it was empty." Finsbury paused, then went on, "I can only conclude that the safe had been burgled some time previously, and that Mitchell by chance came across the diamonds, recognized them, secured them, and was bringing them back."

"I understand he had sent word he wished to meet with Miss Finsbury," Stokes murmured.

Lord Finsbury shifted. "I thought perhaps Mitchell intended to return the diamonds to her in an attempt to regain her favor. I understand they parted under strained circumstances."

Stokes exchanged a glance with Barnaby; on the face of it, Finsbury's supposition might explain why Mitchell had been carrying the necklace.

"If you could clarify, my lord"—Stokes looked down at his notebook —"where were you yesterday afternoon?"

Lord Finsbury remained silent for several seconds, no doubt wrestling with the necessity of replying, but eventually, he conceded, "I was here. At my desk. Busying myself with letters. To be frank, I assumed that when Mitchell returned, he would at least do me the courtesy of looking in and explaining himself. But he never arrived."

Stokes and Barnaby both glanced at the window, confirming that the view ran along the front of the house; the side lawn and the opening of the path from the village were entirely out of sight.

Looking back at Lord Finsbury, Stokes said, "Thank you, my lord. Given the circumstances, I fear we will need to interview each of your guests in turn."

"Merely a formality," Barnaby put in. "And it will serve to ease the speculation, which I'm sure is already rife."

Lord Finsbury had to be well aware of the latter. While he clearly didn't like the notion, he stiffly inclined his head.

"We'll also need to interview your staff," Stokes said. "If you could tell me their names?"

"My sister Agnes runs the household—she will be able to give you the names."

"Is there some private room in which the interviews could be conducted?" Barnaby asked. "Better to keep the experience comfortable and as undisturbing as possible."

Lord Finsbury paused, then somewhat grudgingly volunteered, "There's the estate office. It's a trifle cramped, but it should suit your purpose."

Fleetingly, Barnaby smiled. "Thank you."

He and Stokes rose.

"Thank you, my lord." Stokes nodded politely. "We'll do all we can to conduct our investigation with a minimum of fuss."

"To which end," Barnaby said, "with your leave, Stokes and I will briefly address your family and guests, essentially to reassure them that all is in hand, and that at this point our inquiries are merely the customary formalities and they have no reason to be alarmed."

Lord Finsbury hesitated, then said, "If you think it best."

Barnaby smiled easily. "We do."

Lord Finsbury sighed and rose. "In that case, I believe everyone is presently gathered in the drawing room. If you'll follow me?"

He led the way from the study. Stokes and Barnaby fell in at his heels.

On entering the drawing room in Lord Finsbury's wake, Barnaby eschewed studying the furnishings in favor of studying the assembled company.

Halting in the center of the room, the instant cynosure of all eyes, Lord Finsbury bluntly stated, "As by now you all know, Peter Mitchell was murdered on the path through the wood. This is Inspector Stokes and Mr. Adair, who have been sent by Scotland Yard to investigate Mitchell's death. They wish to speak with you all." Finsbury glanced at Stokes. "Inspector?"

If Finsbury had thought to unsettle Stokes, he'd misjudged; Stokes was experienced in taking command and exerting control in drawing rooms far more exalted than that of Finsbury Court.

Stepping forward to where he could see all those present—and they could see him—Stokes swept the gathering with his gray gaze, then said, "Peter Mitchell's death could not have been anything other than murder. I have been charged with the task of identifying and apprehending his murderer. In order to do so, it will be necessary to interview each of you individually to ascertain what you know about Mitchell and all incidents involving him. Such inquiries are routine and should not be viewed as in any way suggesting that those interviewed are suspected of being involved in the crime."

Moving to stand by Stokes's left shoulder, Barnaby added, "It would also be true to say that such interviews are the simplest way of identifying all those *not* involved." Assuming his most reassuring mien, he went on,

"At this point, there's really nothing behind our questions beyond a wish to gain information about Mitchell."

"Indeed." Stokes reclaimed the stage. "We'll be conducting our interviews in the estate office and we'll ask to see you one by one"—he glanced at his notebook—"commencing with Mr. Frederick Culver."

Both Stokes and Barnaby looked across the room in time to see a tall, lean, athletic-looking gentleman with dark brown hair exchange a glance with the young lady who was standing beside him before the bow window.

The visual connection lingered for too long to be incidental, inconsequential.

For her part, the young lady appeared momentarily oblivious of everyone else in the room.

Then the gentleman looked away—toward Barnaby and Stokes. He nodded. "I'm Culver."

Gently pressing, then releasing, the young lady's fingers, which, Barnaby and Stokes saw, he had been surreptitiously clasping, Frederick Culver walked forward to join them.

Barnaby nodded to Culver and turned to lead the way. Stokes waved Culver on, then followed.

Riggs conducted Barnaby, Stokes, and Frederick Culver to the estate office; Duffet brought up the rear. The office proved to be small but adequate for their purpose, with a decent-sized desk with a battered admiral's chair behind it and two straight-backed chairs angled before it.

After installing Duffet outside the door, Stokes rounded the desk and sat. Barnaby shifted one straight-backed chair to the end of the desk, placing himself in a neutral position, neither with Stokes nor with Culver.

At Stokes's invitation, Culver sat in the remaining chair, facing the desk. He appeared cautious, reserved, but faintly curious, and, tellingly, otherwise at ease.

"Mr. Culver," Stokes began, "can you tell us what you know of Peter Mitchell?"

Culver's features, pleasant, well-formed, but with a hint of steel about his lips and jaw, remained relaxed, the expression in his dark brown eyes direct. "I had never met Mitchell, nor heard of him, until he arrived here on the first day of the house party. That was six days ago. I understand

Lord Finsbury was acquainted with Mitchell, but other than that..."
Culver paused, then went on, "Apparently everyone here other than Lord
Finsbury also knew nothing of Mitchell."

Barnaby frowned. "Rattle didn't know of him?"

"He said not." Culver looked at Stokes. "How did Mitchell die?"

Stokes considered, but could see no reason not to make the revelation
—and several reasons why he should. But first... "I believe you were
aware that Mitchell had sent word that he intended to return to the house
yesterday afternoon, and that he had requested an interview with Miss
Finsbury."

Culver nodded. "Gwen—Miss Finsbury—read out the note—" Culver
paused, clearly thinking back, then went on, "Well, she read out the bit
about him returning yesterday and having something to show her, so
everyone knew that. Later, she showed me the note, and it did say
yesterday afternoon, so, yes, I was aware he intended to return then."

Stokes blinked; would that all his witnesses had Culver's sense of
exactitude. "So where were you yesterday afternoon?"

Culver replied evenly and without hesitation, "Miss Finsbury and I
went for a walk in the shrubbery. There's a break in the hedges and a
bench placed to look out over the side lawn—from the bench we could
see the opening of the path." He paused, then volunteered, "Given the
circumstances behind Mitchell's earlier departure, Gwen didn't want to
meet him alone." Culver met Stokes's gaze. "And I agreed."

Barnaby stirred. "The circumstances behind Mitchell's earlier departure—what were they?"

Culver hesitated; Barnaby got the impression Culver weighed not his
words themselves but rather how they would influence Barnaby and
Stokes's view of the situation. Eventually, Culver said, "Three days ago,
in the afternoon, Mitchell approached Miss Finsbury and"—Culver's jaw
tightened—"convinced her to walk alone with him in the conservatory.
There, out of sight of all others, he attempted to press his attentions
on her."

"But you'd followed them," Barnaby guessed.

Culver nodded. "I didn't trust him—and I was right. Gwen struggled,
but he wouldn't let her go. He tried to kiss her—and that's when I hauled
him off. He took a swing at me, but missed, and I got my arms around
him, trapping his. By then, Agnes had joined us—she'd seen me slip
away and had followed. Agnes had seen what had happened—all of it.
She gave Mitchell a verbal dressing down—I held him while she did it.

Then Gwen slapped him. She was furious. Agnes declared that Mitchell had to leave immediately, and to give the man his due, he agreed to go. I released him and he stalked off. Agnes followed him, and she and Riggs eventually saw Mitchell off in the pony-trap to the village." Culver shrugged. "That's all there was to it."

Inwardly, Barnaby frowned. "You said you didn't trust Mitchell—was there any specific reason for your distrust?"

Culver paused, then, clearly reluctantly, shook his head. "There was nothing I could put my finger on—he was charming and seemed a good enough sort. Easy-going, easy to talk to, yet...there was something just not quite right. I can't be more specific. And, truth be told, if it had been one of the other girls he'd set his sights on rather than Gwen, I probably wouldn't have been so suspicious."

"To return to yesterday afternoon"—Stokes frowned at his notebook —"you and Miss Finsbury were watching the end of the path. Did you see anyone coming out from the path or anywhere in the vicinity?"

"No. And we were watching. We'd planned to meet Mitchell on the lawn, in the open. When he didn't arrive by the time we'd expected him, Gwen and I went into the house to see if, contrary to what we'd thought, the pony-trap had been sent to fetch him, but it hadn't." After a moment, Culver raised his gaze to Stokes's face. "You still haven't said how Mitchell was killed."

Stokes studied Culver's face as he said, "He was immobilized using a trap, then bludgeoned to death with the long-handled hammer from the croquet shed."

Culver's face was akin to an open book as he tried to imagine what Stokes had described. Eventually, Culver frowned. "Trap—what sort of trap?"

Which, Barnaby reflected, was exactly the question an innocent man would ask. "An old-fashioned, steel-jawed animal trap, one large enough to crush a man's ankle. It had been hidden in a dip in the path along a narrower stretch."

Culver looked genuinely shocked. But after a moment, he frowned. "Why trap him first?"

"Indeed," Stokes said. "And regardless of the reason, sadly that means we cannot rule out the possibility that Mitchell was killed by a woman."

Culver appeared even more affronted. A bare second passed before he said, "I cannot imagine any of the ladies of the family, or their female guests, doing such a thing." He looked at Stokes, then at Barnaby. "Aside from all else, as I told you, no one really knew Mitchell. What reason could a stranger have for killing a man like that?"

Stokes stared at Culver for a second, then nodded. "That is, indeed, an excellent question. However, as I said, our inquiries today are purely to learn all we can about Mitchell, and along the way to rule out as many people as possible." He met Culver's gaze. "Lord Finsbury told us you've only recently returned from overseas."

Culver readily volunteered his life history, which was much as Lord Finsbury had related it, and confirmed that it was Agnes, his godmother, who had invited him to the house party.

"Very well." Stokes sat back. "Just one last thing. When Mitchell's body was found this morning, he had the Finsbury diamonds in his pocket."

Culver's eyes flew wide. "What?"

"Do you know of the diamonds?" Barnaby asked.

Culver nodded. "But I haven't seen them in years—decades. The last time was when Gwen's mother was alive—she occasionally wore them." After a moment, in a tone of patent puzzlement, Culver murmured, "I wonder—was that what Mitchell intended to show Gwen?"

Another moment passed, then, frowning, Culver looked at Stokes. "The Finsbury diamonds are worth a king's ransom, but how did Mitchell get the necklace?"

"That," Stokes admitted, "is another excellent question." He glanced at Barnaby, who shrugged faintly, indicating he had no further questions for Culver.

Stokes looked at Culver. "Thank you—you've been most helpful." Somewhat cynically, he added, "I can only hope the others are equally forthcoming."

A quick grin flashed across Culver's face, then they all rose.

Stokes showed Culver to the door, sent Duffet to fetch Miss Finsbury, and returned to his seat behind the desk.

While they waited for Gwendolyn Finsbury, Barnaby replayed and dissected Culver's replies. Eventually, he met Stokes's gaze. "Unless Miss Finsbury is an accomplice, it wasn't Culver."

Stokes nodded. "But what he told us is going to make questioning and assessing the others easier—he's made it clear what questions we need to ask."

Barnaby listed them on his fingers. "One—did they know anything of Mitchell before the house party? Two—did they know he was returning not simply yesterday, but specifically yesterday afternoon? Three—are their alibis for yesterday afternoon vouched for by others? Four—what did they know about the diamonds? And five—did they learn anything at all about Mitchell from the man himself while he was here?" Barnaby paused, then glanced at Stokes. "Is that it?"

"Hmm...most of it." Stokes leaned back. "There's also the matter of access to the foot-trap and the hoop-hammer, but, if I understood correctly, other than Rattle, most of those here have visited many times over the years—they might have stumbled on the trap and the hammer at any time. And, of course, there's all the staff—we have to assume that any of them would have known where to find both items."

Barnaby snorted. "Death by hoop-hammer—that's doubtless a first."

Stokes grunted. "Given the way some of those old ladies play croquet, I wouldn't be too sure of that."

A tap on the door heralded the arrival of Gwendolyn Finsbury. While she was understandably a touch nervous, she made a determined bid to hold her head high—and exonerate Frederick Culver at every turn.

Other than confirming, had they been in any doubt, that she was in love with Culver, her statements added nothing of moment to Culver's observations.

Barnaby resisted the urge to ask Gwendolyn if she had done anything to encourage Mitchell—instead, he asked Agnes Finsbury, Gwendolyn's aunt.

Only to receive a very firm "No." Agnes paused, then added, "I have to admit I did wonder whether Mitchell's polish—he really was very charming when he set himself to it—would sway Gwen, but she never looked away from Frederick, not even for a second. I have no difficulty imagining Mitchell seeing her lack of response as a challenge, but he took things far too far. I was exceedingly grateful that Frederick stepped in."

"Did either of the other young ladies show any susceptibility to Mitchell's charms?" Stokes asked.

Agnes considered, then shook her head. "Not that I saw. Juliet is spoken for, and her mind is constantly engaged with planning her future with Jeremy Finch. As for Harriet, she seems entirely happy with Mr. Rattle and I saw no evidence of any falling out there—and I'm sure I, or Mrs. Pace, or Mrs. Shepherd would have noticed if there had been."

Unlike Culver and Gwendolyn, Agnes had been alone in her private sitting room through most of the previous afternoon, doing the accounts and organizing the coming week's menus. "Given the circumstances of our parting, I had no interest in speaking with Mitchell again, and Gwen had told me that Frederick would stay with her throughout any meeting—and Frederick, dear boy, had reassured me of that."

They let Agnes go. She was replaced by Algernon Rattle, who provided a breath of fresh air with his bright and breezy style, but when they distilled all he said, it amounted to nothing more than confirmation of what their previous interviewees had told them—except for one point. When asked for his assessment of Mitchell, Rattle scratched his head, then opined, "A good enough sort, don't you know, but…well, there was just something that didn't quite sit right. I asked him where he hailed from, and he never quite answered, so I can't help you there." As for the diamonds, Rattle had absolutely no idea what they were talking about; he had no notion a necklace known as the Finsbury diamonds even existed and, patently, didn't really care. As for his alibi, he'd been with Harriet Pace, her mother, and both the Shepherd ladies all through the afternoon.

Rattle was followed in quick succession by all the other ladies, who verified his alibi and those of each other. None of them had succeeded in prizing anything of Mitchell's background from him, but, in the usual way of well-born ladies, all had tried.

Sitting back as the door closed behind Mrs. Shepherd, the last of the female guests, Barnaby met Stokes's gaze. "It's starting to look like Mitchell was being not just careful but obsessive over deflecting all interest away from his background."

"Indeed," Stokes replied. "Which raises the question of why?" He paused, then glanced at a clock on a nearby shelf. "Let's interview the rest of the gentlemen, then see if a break for lunch and digestion results in any fresh insights before we continue with questioning the staff."

Barnaby agreed.

The two older gentlemen had spent the previous afternoon in the library, dozing over the news sheets. Although the conversation had been sporadic, both were quite sure the other had not left at any point throughout the critical period.

On the question of Mitchell, from Mr. Pace they heard, "Asked him if he was related to the Helmsley Mitchells, but he said not. Didn't volunteer much of himself, now I think of it."

Mr. Shepherd was more definite. "I couldn't place him, and when it came down to it, he couldn't place himself, if you know what I mean. I started to wonder if there was something havey-cavey about him—when I heard he'd been murdered, I wasn't all that surprised."

Both men knew of the Finsbury diamonds, but neither had seen the necklace in years, and neither showed the slightest interest in it now, beyond the fact that it had been found in Mitchell's possession.

That occasioned an exclamation from Mr. Shepherd. "Gads! Whoever killed him left a fortune behind!"

"Which," Stokes said, as he and Barnaby rose and headed for the door after Mr. Shepherd had left, "is a fair comment."

Rather than remain at the house and impose on the staff who they would later be interviewing, they ambled back down the woodland path to the village. While they'd been up at the house, the police surgeon's men had arrived and had taken Mitchell's body away, along with the foot-trap and hoop-hammer. A patch of flattened grass and disturbed leaves was all that remained to mark the spot; Barnaby and Stokes skirted it and walked on.

When appealed to, Duffet, trailing respectfully behind, directed them to a smaller tavern which, he assured them, served better fare than the bigger and much busier coaching inns.

Barnaby and Stokes were pleased to approve of the tavern's ale and rabbit pie.

Pushing away his empty plate, Barnaby sat back. "You know, the usual murder has only one mystery attached to it—who killed the victim? In this case, we not only have that mystery, but also a mystery over who the victim was, as well as the joint mysteries of how he got the Finsbury diamonds and why he was bringing them back."

Stokes grimaced. "And given the mystery over Mitchell himself, I find myself less inclined to believe Lord Finsbury's rose-tinted theory that Mitchell somehow stumbled on the diamonds, managed to secure them, and was bringing them back to right his standing with the family. That's too far-fetched."

"Indeed." Barnaby pushed back his chair and rose. "Let's get back and see what the staff can tell us."

They returned to the estate office to discover the neat list of all the staff Agnes had promised to provide waiting on the desk. They started with Riggs. As the butler had already seen the body and knew about the diamonds, there was no beating about any bush.

"I can't say as I took to Mr. Mitchell." Riggs gave the word rigidity new meaning; he sat poker straight, fists on his thighs, and stared straight ahead rather than meeting their eyes.

It was the pose of a proper servant, but Stokes found it irritating. "Why was that?"

Riggs was silent for nearly a minute before replying, "I suspected that he was one of those gentlemen who should not be trusted around ladies, sir. And I was right. I couldn't say I disapproved of Mr. Culver and Miss Agnes throwing the man out on his ear."

"Where were you during the afternoon yesterday—over the time Mitchell must have walked up the path?"

"I was in the butler's pantry polishing the silver."

Stokes glanced at Barnaby, who shook his head. They dismissed Riggs and called in the footman, and in turn the groom, the general-hand-cum-garden boy, and the grizzled gardener. As with Riggs, Stokes put their questions, leaving Barnaby to watch and assess. As it happened, none of the other male staff had any opinion whatever about Mitchell. However, like Riggs, all of them had been alone during the critical hours.

The cook, who they interviewed next, explained, "That's the one time in the day when we've all got a bit of free time to spend as we wish. Lunch is all cleared away, and afternoon tea will either be waiting to be served or already served—it's only Kitty, the parlormaid, who has to tend to that. All the rest of us are free until five, when we start getting things ready for dinner."

The maids who followed—Rhonda, the upstairs maid, Fitts, Miss Agnes's dresser, Polly, Miss Gwen's lady's maid, Ginger, the maid-of-all-work, and Betsy, the scullery maid—were quickly dealt with; none knew anything about Mitchell.

But the appearance of the last maid on their list, Kitty, the parlormaid, who until then had been busy serving afternoon tea, jolted Barnaby and Stokes to attention. It wasn't the fact that Kitty—"Kitty Maitland, sir"—was uncommonly pretty, with rioting blonde curls tucked under her prim cap and a shapely, far-from-girlish figure, nor that her voice was husky and low that riveted their focus. Kitty had been crying.

Barnaby would have taken an oath on it, although she'd clearly made an effort to hide the evidence. More, she was pale and wan, and appeared drained and close to exhaustion.

But Kitty steadfastly denied any knowledge of Mitchell, or of anything else to do with the case.

Reasoning that the source of her upset might be something—or someone—entirely irrelevant to their investigation, Barnaby signaled to Stokes to let her go.

The instant the door closed behind her, Stokes arched a brow his way.

Barnaby offered, "There's no reason to assume that it's Mitchell's death that's so overset her, but her state highlights just how *unaffected* everyone else has been by this murder."

Stokes nodded. "A gruesome enough murder, too. But you're right—no one has shown the slightest sympathy toward Mitchell, which suggests that, despite his oft-mentioned charm, he didn't truly connect with anyone here at all."

Barnaby sighed. "We've interviewed nearly everyone and got nary a hint of any convincing motive." He consulted the list. "We only have the housekeeper, a Mrs. Bateman, to go, and if she's the murderer, I'll eat my hat."

"You don't wear a hat," Stokes replied. "But, regardless, let's have Mrs. Bateman in."

Mrs. Bateman had seen Mitchell about the house, but hadn't so much as spoken to the man, so had nothing to offer in that regard. When Barnaby questioned her about the source of Kitty's distress, Mrs. Bateman shook her head in motherly dismissal. "They all do it—they decide they've fallen in love with some gentleman and assume that he'll fall in love with them, and then they get cast down when he doesn't recip-rocate. Mind you, I'm not saying Kitty had anything to do with Mitchell —it could equally well be Mr. Culver or Mr. Rattle she's set her silly heart on, and no foul to either gentleman." Mrs. Bateman paused, clearly thinking back. "I can't say I ever saw Kitty anywhere near Mr. Mitchell. Indeed, I had hoped she wouldn't be so susceptible, given as she's a touch older than the norm."

Like the other members of the staff, Mrs. Bateman had been alone in her sitting room reading a novel through the critical time.

When, accepting their polite refusal of her offer of a cup of tea, the housekeeper left them, Barnaby and Stokes shared a long glance, then both rose.

"Let's get back to London." Stokes led the way. "The Chief Commis-sioner will want to hear what we've found."

They walked back to Hampstead village, reclaimed Barnaby's curricle, and he tooled them swiftly back to town.

Stokes went straight to the Chief Commissioner's office to report, taking Barnaby with him.

They detailed what they'd found. The Chief Commissioner harrumphed. "Sounds complicated. Clear it up as fast as you can, but keep the whole thing quiet. I don't need the likes of Finsbury griping in my ear."

Thus adjured, Stokes and Barnaby headed downstairs to Stokes's office.

"What's next?" Barnaby followed Stokes into the small room. "Should we list all the players and try to define some direction from the myriad unconnected and mostly irrelevant facts, or...?" Pausing, Barnaby looked at Stokes.

After rounding his desk, Stokes had halted, his long fingers holding down a sheet of paper that had been left, folded, on his blotter.

He'd unfolded it and had been reading the contents.

Stokes grunted. "Dinner." A smile of gentle expectation softened his features. He held out the note to Barnaby. "We've been summoned."

"Ah." Taking the note, Barnaby scanned the few—direct and to the point—lines within, inscribed in his wife's dashing hand. He grinned. "I see."

Picking up the scarf he'd dropped on the desk, Stokes waved Barnaby back to the door. "No sense keeping our ladies waiting—let's go."

Chuckling, Barnaby tucked the note in his pocket and together they made for Albemarle Street.

CHAPTER 3

*P*enelope was so huge she had to sit sideways at the table. Larger framed and two months less encumbered, Griselda didn't have quite the same difficulty, but as there were only the four of them dining, Mostyn and the staff had removed all the extra leaves, reducing the table to a comfortable round.

On arriving at the house, Barnaby and Stokes had discovered their ladies resting by the fire in the drawing room, eager and impatient to hear of the case, to glean all the details. The two men had smiled, sat alongside, at their ease, and obliged, recounting every last little detail of what they'd seen, heard, and, at least where the logic seemed sound, what they'd surmised.

When they'd reached the end of their recitation, with Barnaby capping it with the Chief Commissioner's edict, Penelope and Griselda had exchanged a glance, then Penelope had declared that they would dine before considering the matter further.

Exchanging a look of their own, Barnaby and Stokes had readily fallen in with the direction; rising, they'd assisted their wobbly wives to their feet, then had followed at their heels as they'd made their waddling way to the dining room.

By mutual consensus, they hadn't so much as referred to the case during the meal, but instead had spent a pleasant hour and more talking of Stokes and Griselda's new house, of the adjustments and changes both couples had made and were still making in preparation for the advent of their respective children. For all four of them, this was a personal, emotional, and surprisingly intense time, and it was comforting to be able to share the experience with each other.

But as the covers were drawn, Penelope set down her napkin and looked first at Barnaby, then at Stokes. "Right, then—back to the case. You may bring your sustaining brandies to the drawing room. We'll be much more comfortable there."

After once more helping Penelope to her feet, Barnaby picked up the brandy decanter and two crystal glasses and, with Stokes, followed their ladies' slow progress into the front hall and on into the drawing room. He could easily have carried Penelope and saved her from what was patently a draining—and frustrating, for she was never one to do things slowly— walk, but his mother had informed him that even short strolls were good for Penelope and therefore the baby, and, as he was well aware, there was also the little matter of her pride.

So he reined in his protective impulses and, knowing that, beside him, Stokes was doing much the same, ambled at a crawl in their ladies' wake.

Finally, they were all settled, with Penelope and Griselda seated opposite each other in the corners of the twin sofas nearer the fire and Barnaby and Stokes sitting alongside their wives; their long legs stretched out, ankles crossed, the men cradled glasses of fine brandy in their hands.

Savoring a sip of his brandy, Barnaby waited for Penelope to open the discussion; he had no doubt she would.

Somewhat to his surprise, she started with a frown. "Unlike most cases, where, at this stage, we're usually mining for facts, in this instance it seems that we have a multitude of individual facts, some of which will have relevance to the murder and others which won't, but, at present, you have no way to distinguish which facts fall into which category."

From the sofa opposite, Griselda nodded. "Which facts bear on the murder itself, and which are part of other events going on concurrently at that house party."

"For instance," Penelope went on, "from all you've related, I'm left with the strong suspicion that Lord Finsbury invited Mitchell to the house party in order to play matchmaker—that his lordship was swayed by stories of Mitchell's financial success, and that, in turn, suggests that Lord Finsbury wants his daughter to marry money."

"But," Griselda said, "is that because the family needs money—and given the shabby furnishings, that might well be the case—or was Lord

Finsbury's invitation merely the norm for a father wanting to see his daughter well established?"

"Regardless," Penelope said, "does the reason, the motive, behind Lord Finsbury's invitation have any bearing on why Mitchell was killed?" Her frown deepening, she spread her hands. "How can we know?"

"And then there's the romance between Frederick Culver and Gwendolyn Finsbury," Griselda pointed out, "and also the romance between Rattle and Harriet Pace."

"Indeed." Penelope nodded. "And romance always complicates things —people act in ways they never normally would when in the throes of romance." She shook her head. "Which brings me back to my original statement—with this case, we are swimming in dozens of potentially inconsequential facts, some of which hint at possible motives, but none of which we can yet be sure are actually connected to the murder." Hands smoothing over her distended belly, she blew out a breath, then said, "As far as I can see, we currently have four questions before us. Who killed Mitchell? Why was he killed? How did he come to have the Finsbury diamonds in his pocket? And why was he bringing them back, and to Gwen, rather than Lord Finsbury?"

Barnaby nodded. "That's a reasonable summation."

Stokes stirred and looked at Penelope. "What do you think of Lord Finsbury's suggestion of why Mitchell was returning with the diamonds?" Stokes switched his gaze to Griselda. "That he was seeking to return them to Gwen to regain his position in her good graces?"

Penelope pulled an expressive—impressively dismissive—face.

Griselda firmly shook her head. "Such a construction rests on Mitchell's character being the sort to make chivalrous gestures, and given he had pressed his attentions on Gwen..." Griselda grimaced and met Penelope's eyes. "I really can't see it."

"I can't either." Penelope paused, then shifted, resettling the weight of the baby. "But we need to start focusing on the important facts and ignore the rest, or we'll never get anywhere. Let's concentrate solely on the murder itself—let's see if we can sort out the order of events so we can see what holes we have in our knowledge, and then work on filling them in."

Stokes nodded. "All right. Where should we start—with Lord Finsbury meeting Mitchell?"

Penelope opened her eyes wide, then waggled her head. "I hadn't thought to go back that far, but perhaps you're right. They met at White's?"

"Yes." Barnaby set down his empty glass. "And I can check at the club tomorrow, see if anyone there remembers Mitchell—the doorman almost certainly will—and find out what they can tell me, about Mitchell, and Finsbury, too."

"So Finsbury and Mitchell meet at White's." Penelope took up the tale. "We don't know how often or exactly when, but at least once recently, and Finsbury, impressed by Mitchell's financial successes, takes it into his head to put Gwen in Mitchell's path by inviting Mitchell to a house party—and then Finsbury gets his sister Agnes to organize a house party to suit."

"Which brings us to the day on which Mitchell, along with all the other guests, arrived at Finsbury Court." Stokes consulted his notebook. "That was three days before the day Mitchell left."

"And apparently those three days passed in the usual pleasantry of a typical house party," Barnaby said. "No one sensed or witnessed anything out of the ordinary until Mitchell pressed his attentions on Gwen—"

"Wait, wait!" Penelope waved. "On that point." She looked at Stokes. "The way your interviewees related it, Mitchell deliberately sought Gwen out and inveigled her to walk with him alone in the conservatory. So it doesn't seem as if he was suddenly swept away by passion, but rather that it was a calculated act." Penelope frowned. "Which only raises yet another question: Why would he do such a thing? Did he *want* to be thrown out, because surely he would have noticed that Culver was hovering over Gwen...or was Mitchell such a conceited ass he assumed Gwen would favor him?" Penelope paused, then made a disgusted sound. "As I said, romance complicates things."

Barnaby tipped his head her way. "Yet that's a valid observation, and a question we should bear in mind. Did Mitchell engineer his eviction from the house, and, if so, why?"

"And did any of the above have anything to do with the Finsbury diamonds?" Stokes shook his head. "We're going around and around again."

"Then let's get back to the murder itself," Griselda said. "Regardless of his motives, Mitchell was evicted late one afternoon. He left the house and was driven to the village in the pony-trap, I think you said?"

Stokes nodded. "He got on the coach to London and, as far as we know, traveled all the way back to town. Then, at about midday the next day, Mitchell dispatched a letter to Finsbury Court, to Gwen. The letter was delivered to her at the dinner table and, surprised by the contents, she said aloud that Mitchell planned to return to the house the next day—she didn't specify the time—and that he'd said he had something he wanted to show her."

Stokes glanced at the others. When no one spoke, he went on, "The following afternoon, Mitchell arrived on the afternoon coach from London with, we assume, the diamonds in his pocket. The pony-trap hadn't been sent for him—he hadn't asked for it to be sent—so he walked up the path, stepped into the foot-trap, and fell face down. He must have tried to turn to see if he could release the trap, and the murderer stepped forward and struck him repeatedly in the face with the croquet hoop-hammer."

Penelope blew out a breath; she wasn't normally squeamish, but... "No matter how much of a cad Mitchell was, that was a very nasty way to die. He would have seen it coming." She paused, frowning.

Barnaby said, "The mechanics of the murder raises several questions. Given the path was used by staff as well as guests, and by villagers bringing anything to the house, the murderer took a risk in placing the foot-trap on the path as he did—what if someone else had come along?"

"He would have had to have been there, keeping watch," Stokes said. "Which strongly suggests that he—the murderer—knew that Mitchell was coming by the afternoon coach."

"As far as we know," Barnaby said, "only four people knew that he was coming specifically in the afternoon—Gwen, Culver, and Agnes and Lord Finsbury, both of whom had asked and had been shown the note. However, someone else might have overheard any of them mentioning it."

"But," Griselda said, "the murderer was keeping watch anyway. The foot-trap was just to incapacitate Mitchell. It was never intended to be the murder weapon—the hoop-hammer was."

"Yes! Exactly!" Penelope's face cleared. She looked from one to the other. "That's what's been bothering me—Mitchell's face was bashed in. Not the back of his skull, but his face. And from what you've said, he was struck many more times than necessary to simply kill him."

"His features were pulp," Barnaby flatly said.

Meeting his eyes, Penelope nodded. "That's my point—why? He was known at the house, and was known to be on his way, so it wasn't to hide his identity. Why else obliterate a man's face?"

Stokes blinked. "It was personal. The murderer hated Mitchell that much."

Penelope spread her hands. "You both saw the result—didn't it appear more like a crime of passion? If you hadn't found the diamonds in Mitchell's pocket, wouldn't you be focusing on his personal life to find the motive for his murder?"

Barnaby nodded. "You're right. Mitchell's murder might have absolutely nothing to do with the diamonds."

"Or," Griselda said, her tone dry, "it might." She met Penelope's gaze. "Diamonds can inspire strong passions, too, just not of the same sort. And as we know nothing about how Mitchell came to have the diamonds, there might, indeed, be some highly charged personal relationship involved."

Penelope slumped back and heaved a sigh. "So we're back to an overwhelming plethora of facts, none of which link together in any sensible or indicative way."

"Perhaps." Stokes sat up. "But we now have some idea of what we need to learn—the holes in our knowledge that we need to fill—in order to make sense out of said facts. In order to string them together into a cohesive whole. Or wholes, as the case may be."

"For instance," Barnaby said, "we need to find out whether anyone else knew that Mitchell was expected by the afternoon coach specifically. At present we have alibis for all the house guests over that time, and as we know the murderer had to have been at the scene for at least half an hour if not more, allowing for time to set the foot-trap, then we're left with Lord Finsbury, Agnes, and Culver and Gwen—assuming the latter two were acting together—plus all the staff, although at present we don't know if any of the staff knew when in the day Mitchell planned to return."

Penelope nodded. "I think we can assume that the murderer had to have had knowledge of the time as well as the opportunity. No one at the house could have disappeared for longer than an hour or so throughout the day."

"And there's something else he or she had to have," Stokes said. "They would have had to have had knowledge of the foot-trap—where to find it, how to set it. And where to find the hoop-hammer."

"You said she." Griselda met Stokes's gaze. "Could a woman have set the trap?"

Penelope looked at Barnaby. "Describe it."

Barnaby did.

Penelope grimaced. "It sounds like a typical gamekeeper's trap. Any lady or woman raised in the country would know how to set one, at least in theory. And if you know the knack of it, it doesn't take that much strength. Even an older woman like Agnes could have set it."

"True." Barnaby inclined his head. "But as to where it was, Stokes is right. Finsbury Court lies on what is now the outskirts of town. There's not a lot of game about and Lord Finsbury doesn't have a gamekeeper, although in decades past, he no doubt did. So it's unlikely the trap was simply lying around, waiting to be used, and, in fact, it looked rather rusty and definitely old."

Stokes was nodding and scribbling in his notebook. Closing it, he looked up. "We'd better go. I'm due at the Old Bailey tomorrow over another case, so we won't be able to get back to Finsbury Court until the day after."

Barnaby shrugged. "I'll use tomorrow to see what I can learn about Mitchell."

"And perhaps," Penelope said, struggling upright, "a day away from the scene and the people involved might allow *some* of our plethora of facts to settle into a more recognizable pattern."

"That's happened in the past." Griselda shifted to the edge of her chair. "Stepping back is sometimes the best way to spot the right path forward."

"Amen." Barnaby rose, held out his hands, and when Penelope gripped them, hauled her to her feet.

Stokes stood and helped Griselda up, then the four strolled out to the front hall.

The conservatory at Finsbury Court wasn't large, but that evening it provided a place of quiet shadows and shifting moonlight perfect for the sharing of private thoughts. And personal fears.

"How do you see the investigation proceeding?" Gwen glanced up at Frederick's face. They had slipped away from the gathering in the drawing room; she'd needed to get away from the avid speculation simmering beneath the surface of every comment, every glance, and Frederick had gallantly offered his arm and opened an escape route.

He'd rescued her tonight, just as he had on the afternoon Mitchell had all but attacked her—there, beneath the palms.

She cleared her throat. "I can't imagine who could have done such a thing, can you?"

Frederick remained silent for a moment more, then softly said, "No. I wish I could."

They'd reached the end of the glassed-in room. Frederick halted and turned her to face him. He studied her face, then said, his deep voice low, "I know the most important things I need to know—that you weren't in any way involved and neither was I."

Gwen grasped his hand and pressed his fingers, her gaze steady on his face, on his eyes. "I never for a moment thought that you might be involved—that you could be involved."

He held her gaze, then his lips, almost reluctantly, lifted. "If I'd wanted to murder Mitchell, I would have…I don't know, challenged him to a duel or some such thing. But he wasn't worth it. He wasn't worth risking the future I want—*our* future—for."

They hadn't previously spoken of that future, not in words. Gwen's heart swelled at the realization that all the dreams that Frederick's reappearance had resurrected—dreams she'd thought dead and buried, the fruits of an innocent girl's fanciful imaginings that had never been slated to come true—were his dreams, too.

Her wishes and his matched, were complementary, two halves of one whole, and so if they wished, if they had the courage to, they might bring each other's dreams to life…if they could get past the potential social quagmire of Mitchell's murder.

Frederick saw welling concern dim the brightness of Gwen's gaze.

A second ticked past, then she whispered, "How bad do you think it will be?"

He understood what she was asking; instinct suggested that he utter some glib reassurance, but he could only give her honesty. "I don't know. I expect the intensity of the scandal will depend very much on who the guilty party is, and their motive." He hesitated, then said, "Given no one here had ever met Mitchell before, and your father only knew him via White's and through Mitchell himself, then surely the police must suspect someone other than those here—perhaps someone from Mitchell's past who followed him on his return…" He broke off as he realized the problem with that scenario.

Frowning, Gwen put it into words. "How could anyone from outside have known where to find the foot-trap and hammer?" She glanced up and met his eyes. "They said the hammer was the one from the croquet shed, and, well, where else could the foot-trap have come from? Presumably it came from our barn or one of the outbuildings."

"Perhaps...but perhaps that's not the right question to ask—where those things came from. Perhaps the question that should be asked is: Could they have been easily found by anyone seeking something of the sort?" He paused, then followed that thought further. "What if someone who Mitchell met in London knew he would be coming here, walking up the path that afternoon? What if they came earlier and hunted around? The croquet shed is at the end of the lawn near the shrubbery—easy enough to see and search. And perhaps the foot-trap was just hanging on the barn wall?"

Frederick met Gwen's gaze. "You understand, don't you, that I can't speak with your father about us—that I can't ask for leave to address you, to ask for your hand—until all suspicion of murder has been lifted from me?"

And until all suspicion had been lifted from her father, and Agnes, too. Gwen nodded. "Yes, I know."

"So until this murder is solved, we won't be able to get on with our lives. I spoke with the local constable before he left—it seems the inspector and Mr. Adair won't be returning until the day after tomorrow. The inspector is needed in London, it seems." Frederick paused, then said, "I really can't imagine any member of the house party—either a guest or one of your family—in the role of murderer. Can you?"

Gwen shook her head. "No. And that's not just wishful thinking. I cannot see why anyone would kill a man they didn't really know, especially not like that."

"Precisely. So let's assume that the murderer is not one of us, that he came from outside, from elsewhere in Mitchell's life." Frederick held Gwen's gaze and felt a sense of impatient excitement—the same feeling he'd often had when adventuring—flare. "Perhaps if we can determine where the foot-trap came from—show that it would have been easy for anyone to have found and used—then we might help the police refocus on the real arena from which Mitchell's murderer must hail from—his life away from here."

Gwen's eyes lit; a similar impatient tension thrummed through her fingers where they gripped his. "Yes—that's an excellent idea." For an instant, she held his gaze, then impulsively she stretched up and pressed her lips to his.

Frederick lost his breath. Stopped breathing altogether.

But when her lips remained on his, he couldn't suppress the urge to, very gently, gather Gwen into his arms.

She came—shyly but not in any way reluctant.

He held her like spun glass, drew in a shuddering breath, and angled his head to refashion the kiss—to one of simple yearning.

Something they shared at a bone-deep level. He let his lips firm on hers, let them brush and say all he could not yet say in words.

And she answered.

Gwen stepped forward with no thought beyond her need, beyond an ineradicable desire to share, reassured by the fundamental rightness of the exchange. Their first kiss. She followed the dictates of instinct, pressed her lips more definitely to his and returned the caress, letting her lips speak in this arena where she had no voice. No simple words could describe what she felt—teetering on the cusp of the greatest delight in life —with the promise of a future shared with him shining like a beacon, not just in her mind but clearly in his, too.

The kiss stretched, lips lingering in a wordless pledge—a troth.

They both felt it; both acknowledged it, not just in their minds, but also in their hearts.

When he lifted his head and looked into her eyes, she looked into his, and saw her own commitment reflected in his dark gaze.

Setting her gently back on her feet, he nodded. "Tomorrow. Tomorrow we'll hunt for where the foot-trap came from, and see if, at least for all those here, we can't bring this investigation to a rapid and unthreatening end."

"Damn! I forgot." Lying propped on her pillows, Penelope turned her head toward the large lump in the bed alongside her. "I really hate this, you know. I forget all sorts of important things, and then remember them at the most useless times. I can only hope that my mind returns to its customary incisiveness once this child deigns to put in an appearance."

They'd been in bed for half an hour. The room was wreathed in the usual nighttime shadows. Pushing back the covers, Barnaby turned onto his back, then shifted so he could see Penelope's face. "What did you forget?" He refrained from mentioning that she often remembered things, and just as quickly forgot them again.

Indeed, she looked blank for a second before her gaze sharpened. "Mama—I asked her about the Finsburys. She said they were once much more prominent socially, but, over the last generation or so, they've drifted to the fringes of the ton. You know what she means."

Sleepily, Barnaby nodded. "That fits with all I saw at Finsbury Court. They certainly don't move in the first circles these days. Not quite county only, but sliding that way."

"Yes, well, Mama said that the family's main claim to fame was the Finsbury diamonds. They are apparently unique and quite fabulous, bought from some Russian czar by some long-ago Finsbury for his new wife."

Barnaby's eyes had closed again, but he felt Penelope's gaze on his face.

"Did you get a look at the diamonds?"

He shook his head. "They'd already been returned to Finsbury and he'd put them back in his safe. But your mother's information explains why he was so aghast when the constable brought the diamonds to him and he realized they weren't where he'd thought they were. Learning that your family's claim to fame had somehow walked out of your house without you knowing couldn't have been a welcome surprise."

"No, indeed!" After a moment, Penelope went on, "I don't suppose you could find some reason to ask to see the necklace?"

He wondered what was going through her mind, considered anyway, but eventually shook his head. "I can't see any reason why we might need to see it—at least not at this point."

She made a disgruntled sound, but then settled back once more on her mound of pillows; she could no longer comfortably lie even vaguely flat. "Well, if matters change and the chance arises, do take a peek."

"Why?"

He felt her shrug. "No real reason—I'm just curious."

Griselda lay beside Stokes in their new bed in their new bedroom, in their new house in Greenbury Street. It was a neat town house standing on its own little plot, three stories with a white-painted stone façade and a small garden running all the way around. Iron railings separated the garden from the street, with a gate in the middle giving access to a simple paved path leading to the front porch. The house was the perfect size for them and the family they hoped to have, and it was located just around the corner from Griselda's shop, so she could easily keep her finger on the pulse there while managing her new household.

Smiling, she listened to the sounds of the house settling around them. She'd yet to grow accustomed to the different creaks and squeaks.

Relaxed and deeply content, she waited for sleep to claim her.

And as so often happened when she let her mind roam free, it went around and around, working through the puzzle most recently placed before her, in this case Stokes's latest investigation.

Something—Stokes never knew what it was, yet it never failed to alert him—told him Griselda was awake. Rousing himself from the clinging fogs of sleep, he opened one eye and squinted at her face. Yes, she was awake; she was staring up at the ceiling. "What is it?" His voice was a low rumble even to his ears. "Do you need me to fetch something?"

"No." She glanced at him, lips curving gently in appreciation of the offer. "But I've just realized there's something you haven't put on your list to investigate—an angle we haven't considered."

He blinked; now fully awake, he came up on one elbow the better to see her face. "What?" He'd long ago learned to pay due attention to such insights; there was a reason two heads—or in his and Barnaby's case, four —were better than one. Or even two.

"Consider this. Mitchell left Finsbury Court two days before he returned. He either left with the diamonds in his pocket or he picked them up while he was in London. Setting aside the questions of why he had them and why he was bringing them back to Gwendolyn Finsbury, what did he do during those intervening days in town? Is there any way of learning where he went and what he did? Because, if so, we might then be in a better position to learn the answers to all our questions about the diamonds."

Stokes thought, then nodded. "That's an excellent point. It might not be easy to trace Mitchell's movements but it's worth at least trying to see if we can winkle out any leads...I'll put O'Donnell on to it tomorrow."

"Good." Griselda settled and, her features smoothing, closed her eyes.

Stokes stayed where he was, looking down at her, watching her face as sleep claimed her. She slept, content and happy, beside him every night, and just the thought, that simple fact, still held the power to shake him—to make him feel so much, an eruption of pure emotion.

Add in the fact that she was carrying his child and his heart simply overflowed.

He drank in the moment, savored it—a private moment of unalloyed joy—then he slid back down in the bed, settled beside her and his child, and closed his eyes.

CHAPTER 4

*A*s soon as he reached Scotland Yard the following morning, Stokes sent for Sergeant O'Donnell. The man had worked under him on several cases and was one of those officers on Stokes's list for co-opting. O'Donnell's particular talent lay in appearing unremarkable, and he was thus very effective in extracting information while working out of uniform.

O'Donnell was quick to present himself at Stokes's office door. "You wanted me, sir?"

Stokes waved him in. "I have to spend the day at the Old Bailey, but the murder I was called out to yesterday has a victim whose recent movements I would dearly like to know." Succinctly, he outlined what they knew of Mitchell's journey back to town and his subsequent return to Finsbury Court. "I know it won't be easy, and may be a complete waste of time, but I'd like you to see if you can glean any hint of where Mitchell went when he returned to town. Where did he stay, who with, and did he go anywhere else before getting back on the coach to Hampstead two days later?"

O'Donnell snapped off a salute. "I'll give it my best shot, sir."

Stokes hid a grin. If he managed to catch a scent, O'Donnell would give a terrier a run for its money. "Very good. Out of uniform would definitely be best. I should be back by four o'clock. If you manage to turn up anything, report to me then."

"Aye, sir."

Stokes watched O'Donnell depart, then rose, resettled his greatcoat, picked up the file of evidence left waiting for him on his desk, and set off for the Old Bailey. He would never get used to calling it the Central Criminal Court, no matter what anyone said.

∾

Frederick and Gwen left the breakfast parlor together and took the corridor to the garden hall.

"I've been thinking," Frederick said, "that before we start on the more difficult task of searching for where the foot-trap came from, we should first confirm that the hammer used to end Mitchell's life was in fact the one from the croquet-shed."

Reaching the door that gave onto the garden, he opened it and held it for Gwen. "We last saw the hoop-hammer when Agnes used it to set up the croquet course on the day before Mitchell was killed, but as far as I know only your butler and the police saw the hammer used on Mitchell, so how could they be certain it was the one from the croquet-shed?"

Pausing on the gravel path while he closed the door, then joined her, Gwen arched her brows. "I would have thought they would have checked...but maybe they simply assumed. Regardless, it won't hurt to look." She waved toward the side lawn and the boxlike shed standing against the shrubbery hedge. "The shed is right there."

As they crossed the lawn, Frederick said, "I didn't really look at the hammer Agnes used, but if I was asked to describe it, I would have called it a long-handled sledgehammer." He glanced at Gwen's face. "Is there anything that distinguishes it as a hoop-hammer?"

Gwen grinned. "No—nothing at all. Agnes is the one keen on croquet, but as she grew older she found it difficult bending over to hit in the hoops, so she insisted on appropriating the sledgehammer and using its head to thump the hoops in. Ever since, she's called the thing 'her long-handled hoop-hammer,' so everyone now refers to it as that." Gwen's smile grew fond. "According to Agnes, using a sledgehammer on croquet hoops is simply ridiculous."

Frederick chuckled.

They reached the croquet shed; a simple wooden box about five feet high, three feet wide, less than two feet deep, and held off the ground on short wooden stumps, it resembled an outdoor cupboard on legs. Gwen lifted the latch and swung the door wide.

Directly in front of them sat a long-handled sledgehammer, its heavy steel head resting amid a jumble of hoops, balls, and the wooden mallets used for the game.

"It's still here." Gwen stared at the sledgehammer.

His hands in his pockets, Frederick studied the sight. "Do you know if it's the one Agnes claims as her own?"

Gwen leaned closer, studying the sledgehammer, then straightened. "As far as I can tell, it's Agnes's—meaning the one that's always here."

Frederick stepped back. He waved to Gwen to shut the door. "That means we have both the foot-trap and the sledgehammer to trace." After a moment, he met Gwen's gaze. "Where should we start?"

Gwen's brow furrowed and her gaze grew distant, then her face cleared. "Let's find Penman. He's the older gardener. He's been here since Agnes was young and the estate was much larger—he's the only outdoor staff left who would know what's where in the outbuildings."

"So where do we start in our search for him?" Frederick asked.

They began at the kitchen door and learned from Cook, just coming in with a basket full of freshly-pulled carrots from the kitchen garden, that Penman had said he was going into the orchard to tidy up the leaf-fall.

Frederick and Gwen found him plying a rake beneath the trees.

The grizzled old gardener had expected at some point to be asked about the foot-trap. "I've been thinking on it and I'm certain we used to have several, some of which I know we passed on, but it'd be unlike old Smithers—he was the estate manager in the days when we had one—to have given them *all* away. Always one to look to being prepared for anything, was Smithers."

"So," Frederick said, "the foot-trap might have come from the estate's outbuildings."

"Aye." Penman nodded. "Can't rightly see where else it might have come from. None of the farmers hereabouts would be likely to have cause to use such these days."

"And a sledgehammer," Gwen said. "Could one of those have been found in the outbuildings, too?"

Penman pulled a face. "I doubt it. We keep the big sledgehammer in the barn—still use it regular-like to settle the fence posts."

Gwen blinked. "Perhaps we should check if the sledgehammer is still in the barn. Could you show us where it's kept?"

"O'course." Penman set his rake against a gnarled trunk, then waved them toward the back of the house to where a large barn squatted behind the stables. "Let's take a look."

Frederick and Gwen followed the old gardener into the shadows of the barn.

"Should be over here." Penman led them toward one end of the huge barn. "On its pegs with the rest of the tools."

Rounding the last stall, Penman halted. Pulling off his cap, he scratched his head.

Stopping beside him, Gwen and Frederick followed the old man's gaze to where two pegs clearly set to support some large implement sat empty, leaving a blank space in the neatly regimented row of tools.

"Well, I'll be. P'raps it wasn't Miss Agnes's hoop-hammer that did for the gentleman—mayhap it was the estate's sledgehammer." Penman nodded to the gap. "The one that should hang right there."

Frederick and Gwen exchanged a look, then Frederick turned to Penman. "You said you'd been thinking of where in the estate's outbuildings the foot-trap might have been."

"Aye." Penman turned and beckoned for them to follow. "Let's take a look and see if I'm right."

They followed him through the stable yard and onto a narrow, grassy track that led out and onward, along the edge of some fields.

"Outbuildings are out a ways," Penman volunteered. "This used to be a much larger estate, see, but the master, and his father before him, too, sold off bits here, bits there, until it came down to what it is now with barely an orchard left. But the outbuildings hail from when it was larger, so they're close to our boundaries now. Can't even see them from the house."

Frederick glanced at Gwen and met her arrested gaze. If the outbuildings couldn't be seen from the house, who would have known they were there?

Penman led them past one stone-and-timber building. "Not that one. Least, I don't think so." He nodded ahead. "If I'm remembering aright, the foot-trap should've been in that one over there."

The track they were tramping along had been curving around; Frederick glanced toward the house, at that point hidden behind the high hedges of the shrubbery. The old stone building Penman was leading them to lay tucked back against some trees. More trees grew thickly beyond and to either side of the structure. "Am I right in thinking"— Frederick nodded at the trees—"that that's the edge of the wood?"

"Aye," Penman said. "The path where the gentleman met his end's not that far."

Gwen sent a glance Frederick's way. He caught it and nodded. This had to be it—the place from where the foot-trap had been fetched.

The outbuilding had an old wooden door. Penman pointed to the ground before it. "Been opened recently. See the freshly scraped earth?"

Frederick and Gwen nodded.

Penman released the latch chain and hauled open the door. Inside, the light was poor. They entered and halted just over the threshold to allow their eyes to adjust.

Penman was the first to move. He took three steps forward, then stopped and let out a low whistle. "Well, I'll be." He glanced back at Frederick and Gwen. "Looks like I remembered aright. This is where the foot-trap must've been, and whoever took it knew it, too." He tipped his head toward an area screened from their sight by a pile of old crates.

Taking Gwen's hand, closing his fingers around her cold ones, Frederick walked with her to join Penman. Looking in the direction the old gardener had indicated, they instantly saw what he meant.

Several large plow shares, an old iron trough, and a massive wooden yoke had clearly all been shifted and restacked to one side to give access to a specific spot on the floor. That spot now stood empty, just bare boards where something obviously had previously rested.

All three of them edged past the piled plow shares to take a closer look.

Penman pointed. "See there? Those round spots in the dust are the feet of the trap where the pegs go through to anchor it to the ground. And there?" He pointed to a smudged area to one side of where the trap had sat. "That's where the peg bag was. Old Smithers was always careful with his pegs."

Frederick glanced around, then eased back, drawing Gwen with him. "We shouldn't touch anything—the police need to see this, as near as possible to exactly how we found it."

Penman seemed to suddenly realize what their discoveries meant. "Aye." Likewise avoiding disturbing the dust around where the trap had sat, he followed Frederick and Gwen back toward the door.

Gwen looked back at the pile of old machinery the murderer had shifted to get to the trap. "Well at least we now know the murderer couldn't have been a woman. No woman could have lifted all that."

"Oh, aye." Penman gave the pile a cursory glance, then waved Frederick and Gwen ahead of him through the door. "A man's work it was, getting to that trap."

After agreeing that for the moment they should keep their discoveries to themselves, at least until they could tell the police when they returned the next day, Frederick and Gwen parted from Penman, leaving him to get back to his orchard while they returned to the house via the shrubbery.

Neither spoke, but both were thinking furiously.

Pausing in the garden hall, Frederick caught Gwen's eye. "As far as I can see the location of the foot-trap doesn't only indicate that the murderer is a man, but also that it's highly unlikely that any of the guests could have committed the murder—they couldn't have known the trap was there."

Gwen forced herself to nod. "Or the sledgehammer. How could they have known where that was, either? It wasn't visible even from the barn door."

Frederick hesitated, then in a careful voice said, "We'll have to tell the inspector when he returns tomorrow."

Gwen drew herself up and nodded, stiffly but determinedly. "Yes, we must." Even though that would highlight the fact that the one man who had known Mitchell, had known he would be walking up the woodland path at the specific time, and who could well have known where the sledgehammer and foot-trap were kept was her father.

If her father was found guilty of murder...

Gwen didn't want to think about that.

"Mitchell. Mr. Peter Mitchell?" Jessup, the senior doorman at White's, scrunched up his face in his effort to drag details from his copious memory; his ability to remember patrons was legendary.

Leaning against the frame of the doorman's booth just inside the club's front door, Barnaby waited patiently. It was late morning and the club was open for business, but few gentlemen had as yet passed through its portals; from experience Barnaby knew that this was the best time to seek information from the staff, before they became too busy with the demands of the lunchtime crowd.

Jessup's gaze remained distant but his face slowly cleared. "Dark-haired gent, early thirties, perhaps. Bit on the lean side with a ready smile. Relaxed sort, he seemed. Easy-going." Refocusing, Jessup looked at

Barnaby in triumph. "He came in with Lord Finsbury a few times—couple of weeks ago, it'd be—but I can't say as we know him. He's not a member, and not a regular, either."

Barnaby straightened. "Did you see him with anyone other than Finsbury? Exchanging greetings, any exchange no matter how brief?"

Jessup eyed him with mild curiosity. "One of your cases?"

Barnaby nodded. "Mitchell was murdered two days ago and we're trying to learn more about him. We knew of the connection to Finsbury, but his lordship can't tell us much about the man."

Jessup widened his eyes. "Seemed right chummy when they were here, but that's the nobs for you—begging your pardon an' all. But to answer your question, I didn't see Mitchell with anyone else, but you might try asking Cecil and Tom." Jessup tipped his head toward the interior of the august club. "They were on the bar both times I saw Mitchell. They might have seen him meet with others inside."

"Thank you." Flicking a sovereign to Jessup, who caught it with a grin, Barnaby saluted him and ambled on through the door into the club's foyer.

At that time of day the atmosphere was hushed, almost reverential. Amused, Barnaby wended his way through the smoking room, which played host to a smattering of older gents, some actually snoring. He entered the dining room where several groups of gentlemen were consuming late breakfasts. Some called greetings which he returned, but he didn't pause. The bar lay around a corner off the dining room, and there he found Cecil and Tom.

Barnaby leaned on the bar's highly polished surface, told the pair that Jessup had sent him, and stated his query and his reasons for asking. He described Mitchell as Jessup had.

"Mitchell." Tom frowned. "Was that his name?"

"Ah." Cecil continued to polish a wine glass. "I do remember him with Lord Finsbury, but can't say as I saw him with anyone else. Never heard his name—I did wonder who he was."

Barnaby hesitated, then said, "I got the impression Lord Finsbury believed Mitchell was a member, but apparently not."

"Nope." Cecil shook his head decisively.

"Could he be on the list pending, do you think?"

"He ain't—isn't," Tom said. "We get introduced to those bidding for membership, just so we know who they are. Mitchell wasn't brought around."

Barnaby nodded, pushed two sovereigns across the bar, then digesting all he'd learned, he made his way back through the club. Waving to Jessup, he walked out into the damp chill of the December day.

Halting on the pavement, he took stock. He'd heard of gentlemen like Mitchell before, outwardly respectable gentlemen who gained access to private clubs by passing themselves off as members to legitimate members... "To gain the confidence of legitimate members, in this case Lord Finsbury."

It was entirely possible that Mitchell had engineered his first meeting with Finsbury and built on that. "And if that's the case," Barnaby muttered to himself, "what's to say that anything Mitchell told Finsbury is fact and not fiction?"

A moment passed, then Barnaby mentally shook himself and started walking. There were other people he could ask about Mitchell. No man was an island, especially not in London society, not at any level.

"Finnegan?"

The coachman who had just climbed down from the box of the coach in the yard of the White Hart Inn turned to look at O'Donnell with a certain incipient wariness. "Aye. And who wants to know?"

O'Donnell let his lined, round face crease in a knowing smile. "No trouble. I'm just following up on one of your recent passengers for a friend of mine."

All true, but Finnegan would take the words to mean that O'Donnell was working for one of the underworld crime bosses.

"That so?" Finnegan hesitated, then shrugged and leaned back against the body of his coach. "So what d'you want to know?"

O'Donnell glanced around the yard. Located off Holborn Circus, the White Hart Inn was the terminus for the line of coaches that stopped at the coaching inn in Hampstead village on their journeys up and down the Great North Road. The yard was teeming with passengers, ostlers, coachmen, and guards, and the noise was palpable, but the area around the recently emptied coach was, for the moment, reasonably private. Sliding his hands into the pockets of his nondescript breeches, O'Donnell looked at Finnegan. "Your clerk said you were on the box of the London-bound coach that halted in Hampstead village in the afternoon two days ago."

Finnegan nodded. "Aye. I was."

"My gent got on at that halt and traveled down to town with you."

"Oh, aye—I remember him. The coach was full and the only seat to be had was up on the box beside me. He seemed glad enough to take it." Finnegan returned O'Donnell's regard. "Dark-haired bloke, leanish, tall-ish, gentl'man to judge by his face and accent."

Careful to hide his rising excitement, O'Donnell nodded. "Sounds like him." He paused, then took a chance and asked, "How did he seem to you?" Finnegan appeared to be observant as well as amenable and ready enough to talk.

"Hampstead was our last stop before town so we didn't have that much time to get cozy, but he was in excellent spirits. Grinning fit to burst the whole time and ready to chat as if all the world was going his way—I wouldn't have been surprised if he'd said he'd won the lottery."

O'Donnell blinked; that was not what he'd expected to hear. Tucking the surprising observation away for later examination, he blandly asked, "Did you get any idea of which way he was headed from here?"

Finnegan regarded O'Donnell steadily for several seconds, then, lowering his voice, said, "He seemed a nice enough bloke. You and your friend wouldn't be looking to bring him any grief?"

O'Donnell promptly put his hand over his heart. "I swear on me old mum's grave, m'mate and I have absolutely no wish to harm a hair on the gent's head. We're looking for him more in the way of doing him a good turn." *Namely finding out who murdered him.*

Finnegan studied O'Donnell for another long minute, clearly weighing his sincerity, then nodded. "In that case, I can do you one better than which way he went. He didn't come all the way to the yard. We was caught in traffic and crawling down Tottenham Court Road when he asked if I'd let him off at the corner of Great Russell Street. We're not supposed to let passengers off except at the appointed halts, but we was all but at a halt anyway and he said his lodgings were across the road in Great Hanway Street."

O'Donnell felt as if *he* had won the lottery. "That's"—he could hardly believe his luck!—"a huge help. Here." He hunted in his pockets, pulled out three shillings and handed them to Finnegan. "Have a drink on me and m'mate."

Finnegan accepted the coins with a faint shrug. "Hope you find your gent."

O'Donnell merely raised a hand in farewell and plunged into the crowd. Thrilled to his boots, he made his way as fast as he could to the road.

Great Hanway Street was a mile or two back along the road. Hailing a hackney, O'Donnell called the direction to the jarvey and scrambled in. And grinned.

If he recalled aright, Great Hanway Street was a very short street.

After lunch, Frederick and Gwen managed to avoid all the others and the increasingly open speculation over who had murdered Mitchell and why, and together took refuge in the rarely used smaller parlor.

Although the Holland covers normally protecting the furniture had been removed, the curtains remained half-drawn and the room was awash with the encroaching gloom of an early December dusk.

Her linked fingers twisting, prey to a mounting anxiety she was finding increasingly difficult to hide, Gwen walked to one of the narrow windows and absentmindedly peered out.

The view was of the garden on the opposite side of the house from the wood—but beyond the trees and bushes bordering the lawn sat the barn, its roof visible above the treetops.

Abruptly turning away, Gwen wrapped her arms tightly about her and valiantly battled to suppress a shiver. She failed.

Having closed the door, Frederick crossed the small room and urged her into his embrace. "Gwen—sweetheart."

He didn't say anything more, but he didn't have to; Gwen laid her cheek on his chest and, closing her eyes, let herself draw strength from the comfort he wordlessly offered.

After a moment, eyes still closed, she murmured, "I can't believe that I'm even thinking that the murderer might have been Papa."

Running one palm soothingly up and down her back, Frederick dipped his head closer to hers and quietly stated, "No matter how... unwelcoming, and, let's face it, disapproving your father has been toward me, not even by the wildest flight of fancy could I imagine him setting a trap for Mitchell and then striking him when he was down."

Gwen blinked and opened her eyes.

Seeing he had her attention, Frederick continued, "You *know* your father—you know what he's like. He's often pompous and stuffy, and a relentlessly rigid old stick, and part of that, of the way he sees himself, requires an unbending adherence to the gentleman's code." He paused, then went on, his voice firmer, his tone certain, "He could never bring himself to be such a coward."

After a moment, he felt Gwen nod.

"You're right," she whispered, her fingers curling about his lapel. "He couldn't have—simply *wouldn't have*—done it in that way no matter his reasons. But..." She looked up and searched Frederick's face. "It looks bad, doesn't it? Who else could it have been?"

"That will be for the police to find out, but"—raising one hand, Frederick lifted Gwen's fingers from his chest and lightly squeezed—"with Adair on the case, I believe he'll see the...all-but-impossibility of your father killing anyone as Mitchell was killed."

Gwen gripped Frederick's fingers in return and determinedly drew in a deeper breath. She wasn't normally the anxious sort but she was so worried—and on so many counts. Returning her gaze to Frederick's face, she searched his expression, his eyes, then murmured, "The police might take weeks, even months to catch the true killer, but the story of the murder and the suspicion that Papa might have been responsible will start circulating within an hour of the others leaving here and you know what society will make of the tale in the interim...indeed, even once the real killer is caught. The scandal will be horrendous—the family's standing and Papa's honor will be irrevocably damaged—and no one will care about putting things right even once the truth is known."

Frederick understood her concern, understood what lay beneath it, and knew of only one way to meet the threat. Tightening his hold on her, he locked his gaze with hers. "Scandal is as scandal does, but, regardless, I don't care. I want to marry you, Gwen—I always have and I have absolutely no intention of allowing the actions of some cowardly murderer to steal any of our future—the future I want us to have."

"But society—"

"Is often an ass, and unless you tell me living within it, here in London, is essential to you, if worse comes to worst, we'll simply turn our backs on it." He allowed cynicism to color his voice. "Society may be rabid when talking up a new scandal, but it also has a very short memory."

Looking into his eyes, Gwen felt something inside her ease. "That's true." She paused, then rather shyly asked, "So what do you think we should do?"

"Stay our course." His reply came without hesitation, in a tone that rang with determination. "When the police return tomorrow, we tell them what we've found, then we leave them to get on with their job and we hold ourselves ready to do whatever we need to do to secure our future—the future we both want."

He hesitated, then more quietly asked, "You want what I want, don't you?"

"Yes." It was her turn to answer spontaneously. Lifting one palm to his cheek, she let her eyes speak the volumes her tongue couldn't find the words to express. "Oh, yes."

She stretched up on her toes as he bent his head and their lips brushed, touched, then meshed. Melded as they sank into the kiss, as she parted her lips and welcomed him in, and he came and claimed and she inwardly sighed.

The engagement spun out, the merging of their breaths a heady delight, one that stole the air from her lungs and left her giddy. Left her senses waltzing in pleasure and nascent joy, the caress an unwavering confirmation.

Earlier, they'd shared a pledge, had wordlessly plighted their troth; now they reaffirmed their direction with resolution and determination.

Footsteps approached, heels clicking on the floorboards.

On a smothered gasp, they broke apart—and rapidly smoothed their hair, settled their clothes and, stepping apart, turned to the door as it opened.

Agnes walked in. She looked first at Gwen, then at Frederick. Then one brow faintly arched and she crisply stated, "There you are. The others want to play whist and we need two more for the tables." Turning, she swept back through the door. "Come along."

Like children who had barely escaped being caught in a forbidden act, Frederick and Gwen exchanged a glance overflowing with relief and suppressed delight and obediently followed Agnes from the room.

Stokes had just returned to his office after a day in and out of the witness box when Barnaby appeared in the open doorway.

Glancing up as he sank into the chair behind his desk, Stokes waved his friend to the chair before it.

Barnaby's face gave little away as he moved into the room, but his disaffected slouch as he subsided into the chair spoke volumes.

Somewhat surprised, Stokes arched a brow. "No luck?"

Barnaby's very blue eyes met his. "Mitchell is an impossible man."

Stokes widened his eyes. "What do you mean?"

"No one knows him. No one even knows *of* him. Which, frankly, is ridiculous." Frowning, Barnaby shook his head. "Given Mitchell's age and Lord Finsbury's description of his background and style, I asked everyone I could think of, and I canvassed widely enough that I should have found at least one person—if not several—who knew him or his family, or had heard of him at school, or at university, or at their clubs. I even ran Carstairs to earth and he got me into the army records, but Mitchell never served in any regiment."

Barnaby ran his hands over his face. "In the end, I found Hendon, and Frobisher was there as it happened, and the three of us did a quick and highly illegal scan of the combined ports' shipping logs, but there's no record of a Peter Mitchell arriving over the last months from any of the colonies or from the Americas.

"Oh, and before I forget, contrary to Finsbury's supposition Mitchell isn't a member of White's, nor has he ever been seen there with anyone bar Finsbury himself."

Stokes stared. After a long moment during which Barnaby returned his gaze steadily, Stokes murmured, "It's starting to sound as if—"

He broke off as footsteps came striding along the corridor—not quite running but with a rhythm rapid enough to convey a degree of enthusiasm not normally associated with the more rarefied levels of Scotland Yard.

A second later, O'Donnell, in mufti, appeared in the doorway. He was grinning.

He snapped off a salute to Stokes. "Sir!" O'Donnell nodded to Barnaby, who had swiveled in the chair the better to appreciate his arrival.

Stokes didn't need to ask if his sergeant had anything to report; success radiated from O'Donnell's every pore. Holding up a hand as if to stay the tide, Stokes advised, "Step inside, close the door, then take a deep breath and start at the beginning."

O'Donnell's grin didn't fade as he eagerly obeyed. "I was lucky enough to find the coachman who had driven Mitchell back to London."

Watching O'Donnell settle into a regulation at-ease stance, Stokes reflected that there was no luck about it; there was a reason O'Donnell was one of the best on the force when it came to plain-clothes work.

"I met him—Finnegan—in the yard at the White Hart and he remembered Mitchell well. The coach had been full when it reached Hampstead, so Mitchell had to sit beside Finnegan on the box seat, and according to Finnegan, Mitchell was in excellent spirits, grinning and happily nattering away."

"He was happy?" Barnaby was taken aback.

"Nary a cloud on his horizon, apparently," O'Donnell averred.

"But he'd just been evicted...ah, I see." Barnaby glanced at Stokes. "Our dear wives were correct. Mitchell engineered his departure from the house party."

"Which leaves us to wonder why." Stokes nodded to O'Donnell. "Go on."

"So Finnegan drove back to town but the coach got held up on Tottenham Court Road, and as it was barely crawling, Mitchell asked Finnegan to let him down at the corner of Great Russell Street." O'Donnell drew a portentous breath. "And Mitchell mentioned that his lodgings were just across the road in Great Hanway Street."

Stokes stared at O'Donnell, then shook his head. "You've the luck of the Irish, O'Donnell."

O'Donnell, who was in fact Irish, grinned. "Aye, sir—and you may be sure I got myself to Great Hanway Street as soon as may be. It's only a short street and I found the right lodging house two doors down."

"Thank God!" Stokes tipped his head toward Barnaby. "Adair here couldn't find any trace of Mitchell."

"Well, sir, that's really not surprising because our man's name isn't Mitchell—it's Fletcher. Mr. Gordon Fletcher."

"I knew it!" Barnaby paused, then frowned. "Fletcher. Gordon Fletcher. I've heard that name before..." A second later, Barnaby shook his head and looked at O'Donnell. "You perceive us agog, Sergeant. What else did you learn about our mysterious victim?"

"I spoke with the landlady. Luckily I described the gent rather than asked for him by name, and she didn't guess I was on the force, of course, so she was happy enough to tell me all about Fletcher and his lady-partner, an actress by the name of Katherine Mallard, known as Kitty."

Stokes and Barnaby exchanged a swift glance, but immediately returned their attention to O'Donnell.

"Seems the lodgings are actually in Kitty's name, but Fletcher has been living with her for years and, according to the landlady, Kitty now being past her prime as an actress, she assists Fletcher with his schemes. By which I suspect the landlady meant swindles—that was the inference."

"So what happened when Mitchell—Fletcher—returned four days

ago?" Barnaby asked.

O'Donnell reported, "The landlady saw him come in, happy as a grig, and he told her things were looking up in a big way. When the landlady inquired after Kitty, Fletcher said she was still on the job but would be home in a few days."

Stokes's eyes had narrowed. "Kitty Mallard is presently playing the role of Kitty Maitland, parlormaid at Finsbury Court."

O'Donnell nodded. "Seemed certain she'd be there somewhere."

"Did the landlady know anything more about Fletcher's movements while he was in town?" Stokes asked.

"Not in detail, but she did say he'd gone out first thing the next day and returned before noon, and when he came in, he was frowning. But when the landlady asked what was wrong, Fletcher said that actually things might be better than he'd initially thought. She said he went up to his rooms deep in thought and later came down with two letters. He took them to the post himself, so she didn't see the directions."

"The letter to Gwendolyn Finsbury," Barnaby said. "And another to someone else."

"The last the landlady saw of Fletcher was when he left the house about midday the next day—he said he was heading back to deliver his master-stroke and wrap everything up neatly, and that he expected to be back, possibly with Kitty, in time for dinner." O'Donnell paused, then said, "I decided that as the landlady had told me so much—all we needed to know—that it was worth the risk to see if I could get her to tell me more about Fletcher's schemes. Took a bit of jollying along, but it seems that Fletcher's a flimflam man—very good at chiseling wealthy ladies, young and old, out of their pin money and more."

"*That's* where I've heard of him." Barnaby met Stokes's gaze. "Fletcher's been active for quite some years—I've heard rumors of him and he was, indeed, a gentleman, originally from a good family but an indolent wastrel they'd long ago disowned. The problem was that he was, indeed, charming, and the ladies he charmed gave him their guineas voluntarily—none of the families involved were eager to publicly admit that their young and old dears had been taken for fools."

"Which, of course, is what men like Fletcher count on." Stokes paused, then raised his brows. "But what scheme did he engage in this time that led someone to bash in his head?"

"And," Barnaby said, "did it have anything to do with those wretched Finsbury diamonds?"

CHAPTER 5

Those where the questions uppermost in Stokes's, Griselda's, and Penelope's minds when, after dinner, along with Barnaby, they settled in the drawing room in Albemarle Street to discuss the day's revelations.

While Barnaby did his best to pay due attention to their deliberations, he was prey to an insistent, underlying distraction—one powerful enough to override all else.

For a start, while Penelope was normally a surprisingly hearty eater, he'd noticed that she'd consumed barely a mouthful of dinner, yet she didn't seem bothered, either by the food or her lack of appetite, and she'd been so bright-eyed and enthused while listening to Stokes's recounting of O'Donnell's discoveries that Barnaby couldn't decide whether her lack of interest in food—presumably temporary—was anything to be concerned about.

But then there was her restlessness.

In her usual position beside him on the sofa, she shifted—yet again. Normally she was so focused, her mind so intent on whatever she was thinking, that she remained physically calm, relatively unmoving. Very rarely was she restless.

Over recent weeks he'd noticed that as the burden of the baby she carried grew toward its ultimate stage, she'd been shifting position more frequently. Tonight, she was moving every few minutes.

Yet she didn't seem to notice, didn't seem aware of her remarkable restlessness. Instead, she was happily and patently eagerly engaged in teasing out the strands of their unfolding investigation, her dark eyes bright, her features animated, her voice clear and strong.

Nothing to worry about, Barnaby told himself, and tried to concentrate on the discussion.

"The easiest way to ascertain our progress is to reconstruct what we believe must have happened." Penelope leaned back into the corner of the sofa. "That will highlight the holes in our knowledge most clearly."

Stokes nodded. "How far back should we start?"

"When Kitty arrived at the house," Penelope suggested.

"No," Griselda said, "earlier. What focused Fletcher and Kitty on the Finsbury household?"

Penelope inclined her head. "An excellent point. What was the target of Fletcher's scheme—at least to begin with? Was it the diamonds?"

Stokes raised his brows and looked at Barnaby. "I should think it must have been. If I'm remembering my timeline correctly, Kitty started at Finsbury Court months ago, well before Fletcher introduced himself to Lord Finsbury's notice."

Barnaby glanced at Penelope. "I gather the tale of the Finsbury diamonds would be well-known among the older ladies of the ton."

Penelope nodded. "Mama confirmed it was the one thing they all knew about the Finsburys."

"So," Stokes said, "from one of his old dears, Fletcher hears of this fabulous diamond necklace—"

"And being the sort of scoundrel he is, the details would constitute a definite lure," Barnaby put in. "A fabulous necklace that hasn't been worn for decades and that therefore might not be missed for months, if not years."

Stokes nodded. "So Fletcher and Kitty turn their sights on the Finsburys, and the first step is to get Kitty into the household, which they manage easily enough."

"And, moreover, they get Kitty into the right position," Griselda pointed out. "As the parlormaid in a household of that size, she could move through almost any room, searching at will, without anyone thinking anything of it."

"Exactly." Behind the lenses of her spectacles, Penelope's eyes gleamed. "So Kitty searches, discovers the safe—and then what?" She appealed to the others. "How did they open it?"

Stokes frowned. "Neither Fletcher nor Kitty have any record of burglary, but that doesn't mean that at some point in their respective careers, they wouldn't have learned some of the tricks of that trade."

"Indeed." Barnaby glanced around the circle. "We haven't seen Lord Finsbury's safe, but chances are it's an older type, and for anyone with the right training, opening one of those is simply a matter of knowledge, patience, and access."

A second passed, then Penelope said, "For our present purposes, let's say that Kitty found the safe but that it was Fletcher who possessed the necessary skills to open it. That would explain why he joined the house party—it was the perfect way to spend several nights inside the house."

Griselda was nodding. "And Kitty was there to tell him how best to manage that. In her position she would have heard all the staff gossip— she would have learned that Lord Finsbury was looking for a wealthy gentleman for his daughter."

"Precisely," Penelope said. "The staff always know things like that."

"So Fletcher knew exactly how to approach Lord Finsbury, knew exactly what story to spin to get himself invited to stay at Finsbury Court." Barnaby paused, then went on, "So we have both Fletcher and Kitty in residence, and at some point the diamonds make their way into Fletcher's hands."

"And then he engineers his departure in such a way that no one suspects that he's simply up and left." Penelope arched her brows high. "Actually, that was a very clever move. It left everyone focused on Frederick and Gwen—and I will never believe that when Fletcher pressed his attentions on Gwen, he didn't know that Frederick would be hovering. That entire scene smacks of being carefully staged."

Stokes grunted. "It was a typical chiseler's sleight of hand—make everyone look at the drama over there while he steals the silver—or in this case the diamonds. No one even thought of the diamonds."

"As witnessed by Lord Finsbury's shock when they were returned to him." Crossing his ankles, Barnaby leaned back. "But let's not get ahead of ourselves—Fletcher now has the diamonds and has left the house without raising any suspicions likely to bring anyone after him."

"I can understand why he would have wanted it that way," Stokes said. "If the Finsbury diamonds are even half as fabulous as advertised, Fletcher would need a top-quality fence to handle them, and those gentlemen won't touch any item that's the subject of a hue and cry."

Penelope sat up. "So he needed not just to steal the diamonds but to keep it quiet, presumably for as long as he could—and combined with the fact that the diamonds are very rarely worn, managing to leave the house as he did was utterly perfect for his plans." She wriggled, then settled again. "So that accounts for his excellent spirits subsequently—everything *was* going his way."

"And," Griselda said, "that also explains why Kitty remained at Finsbury Court and didn't disappear at the same time."

"No need to raise questions, even on that score." Stokes pulled a face. "They really were very good at what they did."

"So it seems," Barnaby said. "But we now have Kitty biding her time at Finsbury Court and Fletcher with the diamonds in his pocket in London, and he's all but dancing a jig. What happened next?"

Penelope held up a hand. "The next morning he took the diamonds to his fence...and came back much less happy." She frowned. "Why?"

After a moment, Stokes shrugged. "It could have been one of several reasons—the fence telling him that the diamonds were too well-known to fetch what Fletcher was expecting leaps to mind. Also that he couldn't cut them up because much of the value was in the piece as a whole. We often find burglars left with their loot in their hands and their high hopes dashed, so to speak."

"But," Griselda said, "although deflated...what was it Fletcher said to his landlady? That things might be even better than he'd initially thought?"

Barnaby was nodding. "And later he sent a letter to Gwendolyn Finsbury asking to meet her the following afternoon because he had something to show her—by which he must have meant the diamonds—and the following day, Fletcher set off in good spirits once more, clearly expecting his scheme to end on a high note and expecting to return with Kitty that evening—which suggests that something he learned at his fence's—"

"Or from someone he met while he was out that morning," Penelope put in.

Barnaby inclined his head, accepting the qualification. "True. But regardless, something Fletcher learned that morning made him rejig his scheme. He was no longer going to steal the diamonds, which was why he took them back."

"He was going to use them in some other way," Penelope said. "And given that he had arranged to meet Gwendolyn Finsbury rather than her father, I suspect we can guess what that way was and who had become his new target."

Griselda frowned. "But he told his landlady that he expected to return that evening *with Kitty*. But wouldn't Kitty have been upset if Fletcher intended to transfer his affections to Miss Finsbury?"

"Not necessarily," Stokes said. "Fletcher was a chiseler—convincing impressionable young ladies that his affections were deeply engaged was part of his stock-in-trade, and Kitty must have known that. And, by all accounts, Miss Finsbury has lived a relatively quiet life—she would have appeared an excellent target for Fletcher's charm."

"And yet..." Penelope tilted her head. "Griselda's right. What if, in this particular instance, part of what influenced Fletcher to change his plans was, in fact, that he'd been smitten by Gwendolyn Finsbury? For all we know he might have been—with someone who pretends all the time, how can you tell when they're sincere?—and Kitty, who knew Fletcher so well, might well have realized that he was in danger of succumbing before he left Finsbury Court. Kitty would have heaved a huge sigh of relief when he adhered to their original plan and left. But then how would she have felt when she learned via the servants' hall that Fletcher was expected back the following afternoon, and that he'd arranged to speak with Miss Finsbury?"

"Kitty would have felt very, very uncertain," Griselda said. "She would have tried to meet Fletcher before he reached the house, to find out what was going on and where she stood."

"Indeed." Penelope's eyes gleamed. "So let's say she truly fears the worst, that she suspects Fletcher intends to throw her over for Miss Finsbury and—and we shouldn't forget this point—returning to the social circle into which he'd been born. Kitty is furious. She's a woman betrayed. So she sets the foot-trap, leaves the hoop-hammer in the bushes nearby, and waits for Fletcher further down the path, closer to the village."

"Fletcher arrives." Stokes took up the tale. "They meet and Kitty taxes him with her fears. Fletcher confirms those fears, then, literally as well as figuratively, he puts Kitty aside and walks on—and she watches him walk into the trap, then she follows and uses the hoop-hammer to wipe out his charming—but deceiving—face."

"Oh!" Penelope wriggled. "That fits the facts *so much* better than anything else. I always said this was a crime of passion."

Barnaby didn't look quite so convinced. "I suppose Kitty's reaction—her subsequent distress—might have been the result of a combination of emotions."

"Including," Stokes somewhat grimly said, "fear for her own skin. Murder, after all, is a hanging offense."

"Before we get to the hanging," Barnaby dryly observed, "we need to line up the evidence. We already know Kitty has no alibi for the critical time, and given she's been at the house for months, she might have stumbled across the hoop-hammer and the foot-trap at any time over the past weeks."

"Hmm," Penelope said. "As it's a crime of passion, there won't be any other evidence, not that I can see."

Stokes slapped his hands on his thighs and stood. "We'll need to rattle her." Expectant satisfaction lighting his expression, he met Barnaby's eyes as he, too, got to his feet. "Kitty's had another day to dwell on her actions—let's go back tomorrow morning and see what we can shake out of her."

Barnaby's brows rose as he turned to give Penelope his hands. "It seems we're nearing the end of the case and it's proved to be reasonably straightforward after all."

Grinning, Penelope grasped his fingers and let him haul her upright. "The Chief Commissioner—not to mention the Finsburys—will be relieved."

Griselda stood with her arm wound in Stokes's. "Indeed. And it's only taken the pair of you two days—with our help."

The emphasis she placed on the last words left them all grinning.

With Penelope and Griselda making plans for later in the week and Barnaby telling Stokes that he would pick him up in his curricle to drive out to Finsbury Court in the morning, the four ambled out into the front hall.

Although it was still early, Penelope elected to be wise and retire. She wasn't surprised that Barnaby chose to join her; he would be leaving early to return to Finsbury Court and tie up the case—so he could return to hovering over her.

She didn't need to ask to know that, regardless of the lure of the case, that was his underlying motive.

After he had helped her to disrobe, don her now voluminous nightgown, and then awkwardly climb onto their big bed, she lay back against her small mountain of pillows and, having left her glasses on for the purpose, watched him undress.

When the show was finally over and he doused the lamp and joined her under the covers, setting her glasses aside, she turned his way and focused as well as she could on his face. "Did you ever get a look at the diamonds?"

"No." Turning onto his back, Barnaby drew up the covers. Closing his eyes, he shrugged lightly. "Other than being Fletcher and Kitty's original target, they don't seem all that relevant now."

After several seconds of staring into the shadows, Penelope stated, "I think that, if at all possible, you should try to get a look at them."

Although he was already sinking into sleep, the comment made Barnaby wonder...sufficiently for him to rouse himself enough to ask, "Why?"

"Well..." Penelope half-turned and snuggled a little lower—a trifle closer. Her hand slid beneath the sheets and came to rest, warm and famil-iar, on his upper arm. "I just thought you should grasp the opportunity to seek a little inspiration for the right gift to get me to commemorate the event—and to placate me and restore your manly self to my good graces —when I deliver your heir."

Eyes still closed, Barnaby grinned. "Very well—just for you I'll make a point of getting a look at the fabulous Finsbury diamonds."

She patted his arm and lay back. "Good."

Silence fell. Even as sleep drew nearer, attuned to her as he was, he sensed her relax and—somewhat surprisingly—fall asleep without any further wriggling and restless shifting.

The ease of her slumber soothed and reassured him.

Inserting a note into his mental diary to make an appointment to discuss diamonds with Aspreys, Barnaby let Morpheus claim him.

"Murder casts such a long and dark shadow." Arms tightly crossed, Gwen stood at the end of the conservatory and looked out at the night-shrouded garden.

Having followed her into the glass-encased space, unlit but for the faint, silvery light of the waning moon, Frederick strolled past the leathery fronds of a palm to halt by her side.

He studied her profile, limned by the moonlight. Murmured, "True enough, but until we know who the murderer is, there's little we can do, and no reason to suppose that that shadow will fall on us." He paused, then added, "I really don't believe your father was involved, not in any way, with Mitchell's death."

"I don't want him to be, but how can we be sure?" Gwen hugged herself harder. "You saw him this evening—he was more distracted than I've ever seen him."

Frederick couldn't refute that; his prospective father-in-law had been unnaturally tense all evening, almost jittery. Indeed, exactly as if he feared being found out...Frederick frowned. "We don't know what might be behind his agitation. It could very well be something business-related." He could recall as if it were yesterday his own father's strikingly similar behavior just before Frederick and his mother had learned of the massive losses his father's investments had sustained.

And the people whose reaction his father had feared the most? Frederick and his mother.

"Whatever it is," Frederick said, "he'll need his family behind him, not doubting him." He knew that from experience; his mother had staunchly stood shoulder to shoulder with his father in facing the ramifications of their sudden and so unexpected descent into poverty, and, at least in Frederick's eyes, that had made all the difference. Despite their severely straitened circumstances, his parents had lived out the rest of their lives in happiness and peace.

They had also encouraged him in his own endeavors and had lived long enough to know of his success. They'd been so proud of him, and he'd been proud of them. The Culvers were survivors.

But now he was the only twig left on his branch of the family tree and he wanted—needed—to put down roots and grow a family of his own.

Reaching for one of Gwen's hands, he twined his fingers with hers and tugged her arm from around her middle. Smoothly, he drew her arm up and out, then gathered her in, much as he would if they'd intended to waltz. He held her like that, as if poised to step out and sweep her away; looking down into her face, he saw her lips reluctantly lift.

She held his gaze. "You're trying to distract me."

"Is it working?"

The curve of her lips deepened, then a soft laugh escaped her. "Actually, it is. I find it hard to think when in your arms, and if I think at all, it's about you and me." She paused, then added, "About our future."

"Good." Setting her raised hand on his shoulder, he closed his arms lightly around her. "Thinking about our future is to be encouraged."

She arched a brow. "In that case, tell me about your adventures in Africa—it sounds highly romantic."

He laughed cynically. "That's the last thing it was. But there were some nice places—perhaps I'll take you to see them sometime."

She tipped her head, studying his eyes. "You don't want to return there to live?" *After we're wed.*

He heard the words she didn't say. He shook his head. "No. I still hold a controlling interest in the company and will need to check on it from time to time, but I left good staff in charge, and two other shareholders, too, to keep watch on things." Holding her gaze, he said, "I inherited my parents' house and I've reacquired much of the land my family used to have." He tipped his head outside, to the north; his home lay in the next valley. "I want to see what I can make of that—I have visions of becoming a country gentleman with my wife entertaining the vicar in the drawing room and a brood of children playing in the garden."

Gwen didn't say anything for several seconds, too busy drinking in the sincerity that shone so clearly in his eyes, the open honesty of his feelings on display for her to see. Finally drawing a breath, she said, "So you have the house and land—might I suggest you concentrate on your wife next?"

"I intend to." His voice had deepened. His gaze roamed her face; despite the blatant invitation he must have seen in her eyes, she sensed him hesitate, then he locked his gaze with hers and said, "I know that no matter how much I distract you, you still worry that, should your father somehow be involved in Mitchell's murder, the consequent scandal will come between us—that because of it I will pull away." He paused, and she felt the full weight of his dark gaze. "I want you to know that that will never happen." Briefly, he shook his head. "During all the years I toiled in Africa—and at first it was true toil and struggle—the one thing that kept me going through the lonely years and through all the hardships was thinking—dreaming—of you. When I was finally able to come home, I hardly dared hope that you would still be free—yet there you were, and it seemed as if fate had decreed it—that you were truly meant for me."

"I am." Through the shadows she held his gaze. "I've always known that."

His smile was fleeting, fading as he searched her eyes and realized she'd meant the words literally. "You have?"

Realization struck, and Frederick had to pause to drag in another breath, to hold the welling euphoria at bay long enough to address the one remaining hurdle. "It seems," he said, his voice low, "that you and I are in accord, yet I know your father wishes you to marry well—to put it bluntly, to marry a fortune."

"My father may wish that, but I don't." Gwen's gaze remained steady on his. "And if we're exchanging reassurances, let me state categorically that having learned that the man I spent all my girlhood dreaming of marrying has spent those same years dreaming of marrying me, I fully intend to marry him—if he'll have me—come what may."

Frederick caught the hand at his shoulder and, his eyes locked with hers, raised it to his lips. "Come what may, that man will marry you, Gwendolyn Finsbury."

She smiled somewhat mistily. "We're a good match it seems. And just to be clear on the issue, I would marry you were you the meanest pauper and—please do note—I was perfectly prepared to return to Africa with you, and I will should that be in our cards." She paused, then said, "After all that I've seen and observed in our world, I know that there's only one thing that truly matters in a marriage—and it's one thing we have, one thing I am determined to seize and hold onto with every last iota of passion in my soul."

His answering smile made her heart turn over. "And I'll be there, by your side, clinging to the same thing, with the same passion, through hell or high water." Lowering his head, he whispered across her lips, "Come what may."

She kissed him and he kissed her, and in unquestioning accord both relinquished the last shield, the last barriers—let them fall.

And set their passions free, unrestrained, and with joyfully greedy delight, let the caress escalate.

Encouraged, he drew her flush against him. Emboldened, she clasped one hand about his nape and speared the fingers of her other hand through his silky hair.

She clung as his tongue stroked heavily over hers and her toes curled.

Together, they plunged into the heat, into the whirlpool of their senses. Into the exquisite sensations sparked by spiraling desire.

A touch here, a lingering caress there, and nerves tightened, breaths shuddered.

"I love you," she whispered, her palm cradling his cheek.

"And I love you." His voice was nearly guttural. "I always will, until my dying day."

Those were the last words they needed, the last that were relevant.

Passion claimed them and touch became their language, desire their beacon, and shared pleasure their mutual goal.

Yet beneath the heat and the rising tide of yearning, their "one thing" thudded like a heartbeat, steady and strong.

A reassurance and a guarantee, a talisman for the future.

An indisputable promise that their dreams could become, and would become, reality.

In the soft dark of the conservatory with the eternal moon as witness, they confirmed, reaffirmed, and pledged themselves to each other, to the future they were determined to seize, to share, to live.

Come what may.

CHAPTER 6

A wife who understood one, Barnaby reflected, was worth her weight in gold. Or even diamonds.

Despite Penelope looking rather wan and unusually drawn that morning, when he'd offered to remain and perhaps read to her, she'd looked at him for a moment, then simply said, "You should go with Stokes. He'll need you to close the case, and we're obviously at that point where everything suddenly becomes clear—you need to be there, not here."

He'd hesitated for a fleeting instant, then he'd smiled gratefully, stooped to kiss her lips, and driven off to fetch Stokes.

Only to discover that Stokes, now anticipating an arrest, had decided to take two constables along and had commandeered a Yard coach and driver. After dispatching a message to Connor, his groom, to come and fetch his curricle from Stokes's house, Barnaby had joined Stokes and the constables in the capacious coach for the journey to Finsbury Court.

Now, climbing the front steps of the house shoulder to shoulder with Stokes, Barnaby had to admit that he felt the same rising expectation of a swift and neat outcome as Stokes did.

Duffet stood waiting by the front door. "Sir." He saluted Stokes, tugged the bell chain, then shifted to take position behind Stokes and Barnaby, with the two constables from London flanking him.

On being admitted by Riggs, Stokes asked to see Lord Finsbury. While Riggs went to ascertain his master's availability, Stokes instructed the three constables to remain in the front hall. "And keep your eyes open."

A moment later, Riggs returned and conducted Stokes and Barnaby to his lordship's study.

Lord Finsbury looked well on the way to haggard, but he rose and greeted them politely, then waved them to the chairs before his desk. Looking past them as he sat, he frowned. "That will be all, Riggs."

From the corner of his eye, Barnaby saw the butler, who had hovered before the partially closed door, bow and retreat, closing the door behind him.

Lord Finsbury clasped his hands on his blotter. "What news, gentlemen?"

Barnaby sat back and let Stokes take the lead in informing his lordship of the true identity of the man his lordship had known as Peter Mitchell, and of all they'd surmised of Mitchell-Fletcher's plans to steal the Finsbury diamonds. The name Katherine Mallard clearly meant nothing to Lord Finsbury, but there was no reason he would have heard his parlormaid referred to by any name other than "Kitty."

Having detailed the plan while referring to Kitty only as Fletcher's accomplice, Stokes concluded with, "We believe that Fletcher's accomplice within the household was his longtime lover, Miss Mallard, who we suspect is Kitty Maitland, one of your maids."

"*Kitty?*" Lord Finsbury looked shocked. "Good gracious! She dusts in here...well, I suppose that's how Mitchell knew..."

His words trailed away. After a moment, he frowned. He hesitated, but then asked, "Do you have any idea why Mitchell—Fletcher—was bringing the necklace back?"

"As to that," Stokes said, "we can only guess, but perhaps if we have a word with Kitty herself, we might get to the truth."

Finsbury blinked. For a moment, he looked as if he wanted to argue, but then, slowly straightening, he leaned back and reached for the bellpull hanging against the wall behind the desk. "Do you think she knows who killed Fletcher?"

"Actually," Stokes replied, "at the moment we're entertaining the possibility that Kitty herself killed her lover."

Lord Finsbury looked even more horrified—presumably at the thought of his household harboring a homicidal female. He looked up as Riggs came into the room. "Our parlormaid, Kitty, Riggs—please fetch her. The inspector wishes to speak with her."

Riggs bowed and departed.

The minutes ticked by. Lord Finsbury frowned and tapped his fingers on his blotter, drawing Barnaby's attention. Noting that, Lord Finsbury stopped tapping; after a second's hesitation, he clasped his hands on the desk. Barnaby pretended he hadn't noticed anything. Beside him, Stokes sat silent and still, a predator patiently waiting for his prey.

After a good ten minutes, Lord Finsbury lost patience; scowling, he tugged the bellpull again.

When Riggs appeared, his lordship barked, "Well? Where is she?"

Barnaby and Stokes turned to look at the butler.

Riggs appeared rattled. "I'm afraid I can't say, my lord. No one has seen Kitty recently, not for an hour or so. But she must be here some-where—I've set the others searching."

"Well, search faster!" Lord Finsbury glared. "I want her found and brought here immediately."

"Yes, my lord." Riggs beat a hasty retreat.

A tense silence descended.

Lord Finsbury shifted, then with obvious reluctance asked, "Should we inform the guests, Inspector? Put them on their guard? I wouldn't want any of them to find themselves in danger."

Stokes considered, then replied, "I doubt that Kitty poses a threat to anyone else, my lord, and I can't see that creating a panic is likely to help, but if you deem it wise to inform your house guests...I must leave that decision to you."

Lord Finsbury grimaced. After a moment, he murmured, "Perhaps we should wait to see if Riggs and the others find her."

Barnaby wasn't sure where the idea that popped into his head came from, but the impulse to act on it was too strong to resist. And where was the harm? He glanced at Stokes. "I'm just going to have a word with Duffet."

Stokes swiftly searched his eyes, then nodded. "I'll wait here. If you have any errands, he and the other two are yours to command."

Barnaby suppressed his appreciative grin, rose, and, with a noncommittal nod to his lordship, let himself out of the study.

He strode back to the front hall. A few quick words sent Duffet and one of the other constables off at a run.

Returning to the study, Barnaby resumed his seat.

Stokes arched a brow at him.

"All taken care of." Settling, Barnaby sat back to await developments.

The first of which was the reappearance of Riggs, who burst into the study in a most un-butler-like state. His hair looked like he'd run his hands through it—several times. "My lord, we can't find Kitty anywhere in the house. We believe she must have gone for a short walk and met with some accident. Perhaps nothing more than a sprained ankle, but with a murderer on the loose, who knows? With your leave, my lord, I believe we should mount a search. Penman and Dobbins have already gone out, so we only have Carter and Percy to help." In a fret of agitation, Riggs glanced at Stokes. "Perhaps the inspector's men might assist us?"

Transparently thrown off-balance by the unexpected turn of events, Lord Finsbury looked to Stokes for direction.

Barnaby seized the reins. "As we need to speak with Kitty..." Uncrossing his legs, he rose. "Where do you suggest we should search?"

Stokes shot Barnaby a penetrating look, but followed his lead and murmured a general assent. They waited while, at Riggs's urging, Lord Finsbury extracted a map of the estate and surrounds from a sideboard drawer and spread the map over the desk.

Gathering around, the four of them studied the map.

Riggs pointed to the representation of the shrubbery. "That's the most likely place she would have gone for a quick walk. And if she went further..." His finger traveled on toward the fields beyond the house— away from the wood and Hampstead village. "That's where she would have gone."

Barnaby saw no harm in asking, "Not toward the village?"

Riggs shook his head decisively. "No. She had no reason to go that way." He paused to draw a steadying breath. "And we—the staff—tend to avoid that side of the house because the guests are often on the lawn, or in the rooms looking out that way."

A reasonable enough answer, but pieces of a jigsaw that showed quite a different picture to the one Barnaby had started out with that morning were starting to slide into place in his mind.

"My lord, with your permission, I'll go out with Carter and Percy to the shrubbery." Riggs glanced at Stokes. "And if the inspector will send his men out to the fields, perhaps we can cover the ground more rapidly."

Stokes made a noncommittal sound and, unhelpfully to Riggs, continued to study the map. After a moment, Stokes pointed to the area before the house. "What lies this way?"

The window of Lord Finsbury's study afforded a view along the front of the house. A flicker of movement at the edge of his vision had Barnaby lifting his head to look past Stokes and out of the window.

Stokes glanced at him.

Barnaby's lips lifted in a small, coolly satisfied smile. Briefly, he met Stokes's inquiring gaze, then tipped his head toward the window. "I believe our search is redundant."

Stokes and Lord Finsbury turned to look.

Barnaby watched as Riggs followed suit—and took in the sight of Kitty Mallard being marched to the house, her arm firmly gripped by one of Stokes's burly constables. Kitty was wearing her hat and coat; Duffet, walking on her other side, was carrying a battered traveling bag.

From their direction it was clear they'd come up the path from the village.

Even from a distance, Kitty looked pale and almost as haggard and worn down as Lord Finsbury.

What interested Barnaby even more was Riggs's reaction—the blood drained from the butler's face and he all but visibly deflated. Just for an instant, desperation stood clearly etched on his features, but then he drew in a breath, straightened, and his usual, rather stone-faced butler's mask slid back into place.

Kitty and the two constables were admitted to the house. Seconds later, a brisk knock sounded on the study door.

Still standing somewhat stunned behind his desk, Lord Finsbury called, "Come."

The constable who had remained on duty in the front hall looked in. He dipped his head to his lordship, but addressed Stokes. "Sir—the others want to know where you want Miss Mallard."

Stokes glanced at Lord Finsbury. "With your permission, my lord, Mr. Adair and I will interview Miss Mallard in the estate office."

His lordship nodded. "Yes, of course."

Stokes looked at the constable. "Where did they find her, Jones?"

Jones nodded at Barnaby. "Right where Mr. Adair thought she would be—at the coaching inn waiting for the London coach to come in. Phipps said they got there just in time—another five minutes and she would have been away."

Stokes humphed.

With a brisk salute, Jones closed the door.

Stokes turned to Lord Finsbury. "By your leave, my lord, we'll interview Miss Mallard, and with luck we'll have the case solved within an hour and be able to leave you and your guests in peace. Perhaps you might reassure them that all is in hand?"

Slowly, Lord Finsbury nodded. "Thank you. I will."

"I will report on our progress before we quit the house." With a graceful nod, Stokes turned and, collecting Barnaby with a look, strode to the door.

Rapidly parting from his lordship, Barnaby followed Stokes. The estate office lay toward the back of the house off a different corridor from the front hall. Returning to the hall and discovering Jones still hovering by the front door, Stokes paused to confirm he wanted Jones to remain on duty there. "Just in case."

Not yet sure how to align the most recent puzzle pieces he believed he'd now discerned, Barnaby walked beside Stokes toward the estate office. Coming within sight of the door and seeing Duffet standing guard outside it, Barnaby murmured, "It might be wise to ask Duffet to take special note of anyone who tries to approach the office on whatever pretext."

Stokes slanted him a glance. "The butler?"

Barnaby shrugged. "There's something there, but exactly what, and how it ties into everything else, I'm not yet sure."

Stokes's gaze turned long-suffering. "Just tell me when you are."

Barnaby grinned.

Stokes paused to give Duffet the suggested instruction, then led the way into the room.

Kitty Mallard had stopped crying, but the evidence of grief—whether compounded by guilt or not—lay deeply etched on her face. But Kitty wasn't a silly young thing; she was at least thirty years old, mature and experienced, and she knew the ways of her world.

She sat in the chair before the desk in the pokey estate office, with Phipps, Stokes's other constable, standing at attention at her back. She'd removed her bonnet and unbuttoned her coat. With her bonnet in her lap, she watched with no apparent emotion bar resignation as Stokes settled in the chair behind the desk and Barnaby sat in the chair to Stokes's right, angling the chair the better to observe Kitty's face.

Stokes met Kitty's gaze, read the weariness therein, took in the defeated slump of her shoulders. After a moment, he said, his tone mild,

"Perhaps, Miss Mallard, we might start with the question of why you took the position of parlormaid in this household."

Kitty met his gaze directly. When she spoke, her voice was low—lower than it had been two days before—and faintly hoarse. "Fletcher. It was a part of his plan." She paused, her gaze growing distant, then continued, "He'd heard of the Finsbury diamonds from some of his old dears several times over the years. He was growing older and he knew he wouldn't have much longer in the game." Her lips twisted cynically. "Charm will only go so far once the handsomeness fades."

She drew an unsteady breath and went on, "So he decided to try for the diamonds. It wasn't our usual caper, which we figured would help keep the police off our necks, but in his wilder days Fletcher had learned to crack safes, so...he set to and ferreted out all he could about the Finsburys, but it quickly became clear that, with one thing and another, we needed information from inside the house. That was always my role. Fletcher came to the village and persuaded the silly thing who was parlormaid before me into leaving for a better post. Easy enough to arrange through an agency in town, and then I stepped in."

In a tone that held little animation, Kitty led them through her surreptitious searching; as she kept mentioning, it had all been very easy. Locating the safe, sending word to Fletcher of the make and type. "And, of course, I learned all I could from the staff. It was common knowledge Miss Agnes and Lord Finsbury had a difference of opinion over Miss Gwendolyn and who she should marry. Miss Agnes was all for giving her time to find the right gentleman while his lordship wanted her to marry money, and soon. He'd got a tick in his ear about looking further afield than the local gentry—looking at gentlemen who'd made their fortunes through investments and business in the colonies and such." Kitty paused, then said, "I wrote it all down for Fletcher—the role was all but tailor-made for him."

Kitty's lips curved slightly in faint, clearly fond, reminiscence; Stokes glanced at Barnaby and gave Kitty a moment to savor the past before he prompted, "So Fletcher bumped into Lord Finsbury, introduced himself, and put himself forward as the perfect candidate for Miss Finsbury's hand."

Her smile deepening a fraction, Kitty replied, "You're not giving him enough credit—smooth as silk, he was. I told him what days his lordship went to town and that his club was White's. Fletcher would have had no trouble—he'd done it before, getting into friendships with gentlemen to gain access to ladies of their families. That way, the ladies see him as someone their nearest and dearest have vouched for—gains their trust instantly, you see."

"As it did in this case," Barnaby murmured. "No one questioned Fletcher's bona fides when, as Mitchell, he joined the house party."

Kitty nodded and drew in a deeper breath. "He settled in quick, and two nights later he opened the safe and took the diamonds. He showed them to me the following day. Absolutely fabulous, they were, winking in the sunshine."

Stokes asked, "Why didn't the two of you leave then? You had what you'd come for."

Kitty snorted derisively. "We weren't such fools. If we'd done that—just cut and run—suspicions would have been raised, his lordship might have checked his safe, and then there would have been a hue and cry over the diamonds, and quite aside from that cutting their immediate value to next to nothing, you'd have known who was responsible and you'd have had us in your sights. Fletcher and I were always careful to avoid focusing attention on us."

"That's why he engineered the scene with Miss Finsbury and Culver that got him ejected from the house party," Barnaby said.

Kitty nodded. "Just shows what an artist Fletcher was—he needed to leave with an excuse no one would question, and there was Culver hovering like a dog over a bone with Miss Finsbury. The very Miss Finsbury his lordship wanted Fletcher to court. It couldn't have been more perfect."

"So Fletcher got himself thrown out and left. All that was a part of your plan." Stokes met Kitty's washed-out hazel eyes. "When were you supposed to follow him?"

"Not for another week or so." Kitty paused, then said, "We talked about it and decided I would need to stay for at least a week after the house party. We didn't want anyone connecting my leaving with him."

"So why," Barnaby asked, "did Fletcher come back?" He remembered the second letter Fletcher had sent. "He wrote to you, didn't he?"

Frowning, Kitty nodded. "It arrived with the letter to Miss Finsbury, but all Fletcher said was that there'd been a change of plans. He said not to worry, that if anything this scheme looked set to be even better than we'd imagined. He told me he'd come and meet with Miss Finsbury and possibly his lordship, and that he'd meet me in the shrubbery when he was done and he would explain all then."

Stokes eyed Kitty consideringly. "Do you have his letter?"

Kitty grimaced. "I burnt it. Too incriminating to keep it, not that it said much."

Stokes glanced at Barnaby, caught his eye, then Stokes returned his gaze to Kitty. Leaning forward, he rested his forearms on the desk and clasped his hands. "Miss Mallard, let me put one possible explanation of all the facts to you."

Kitty eyed him warily.

"We all agree that Fletcher arrived here as a guest for the house party, and that subsequently he took the diamonds from Lord Finsbury's safe—as per your original plan. But what if, during those days here, Fletcher met and grew enamored of Gwendolyn Finsbury. He still took the diamonds and went through with your scheme, but, when he got to London and had the necklace valued…perhaps he wondered if there was a better way forward. One that involved him bringing the necklace back to Gwendolyn Finsbury, spinning some tale that he'd found it in town, and using it as a means to get back into her good graces—and those of her father. And, of course, as reward for returning such an important set of jewels to the family, he would claim Gwendolyn's hand. In such a scenario the letter he sent to you—which you subsequently destroyed—said something quite different. Fletcher told you he intended marrying Miss Finsbury…and where did that leave you? Angry, no doubt—furious, even. Perhaps furious enough to set that foot-trap on the path, and when he stepped into it, to beat your ex-lover to death."

Kitty had grown paler and paler, but her eyes never left Stokes's. Now, her face set, she simply stated, "No. That didn't happen." She glanced at Barnaby and her lips twisted in a scoffing expression. "It may not be how things are done in your world, but Fletcher and I had been together for more than a decade, living together and working together." She looked at Stokes and her gaze was steady. "We might never have tied the knot officially, but it was the same thing."

Easing back in her chair, she drew a deeper breath, then went on, "And, if you please, what possible use would Miss Finsbury be to Fletcher? He had no money to speak of, and the Finsburys aren't wealthy or his lordship wouldn't be looking for a wealthy husband for his daughter. Fletcher was thirty-five. He'd lived life and was cynical to his toes. The chances that he'd had his head turned by Miss Finsbury—over a span of a few days at a house party—aren't big enough to point to."

In Stokes's experienced assessment, Kitty was speaking the truth. She was also an ex-actress. Still holding her gaze, he said, "Maybe it was you who wanted to move on and you had to get rid of Fletcher to do so. Perhaps, contrary to what you've told us, you were supposed to leave with him, or at least follow him back to London the next day, but when you didn't show…he wrote those two letters. One to Miss Finsbury arranging a mysterious meeting to act as his excuse for returning to the house, and a second letter to you, asking you to meet him. Perhaps he brought the diamonds to help persuade you to return with him to town. But you didn't want to continue with him and that life, so you trapped him on the path and—"

Kitty stayed him with an upraised hand; this time her expression was all scornful disgust. "Before you suggest that I bludgeoned Fletcher—my lover of ten and more years—to death, just answer me this. If I was intending to break with Fletcher, who was I leaving him for?"

Increasingly belligerent, Kitty looked from Stokes to Barnaby. Brows rising, she spread her arms and demanded, "Who? Lord Finsbury? Culver? Rattle? Or perhaps old Riggs? Admittedly he'd have me, but why on earth would I want to end up here, stuck in a country backwater, when with Fletcher I lived within a stone's throw of Leicester Square?"

Barnaby met Stokes's gaze. For a woman of Kitty's background, that last point was difficult to argue.

But that left them with the question: If not Kitty, then who?

"No answer?" Kitty prompted. When they looked at her but said nothing, she snorted and folded her arms. "It wasn't me—get that through your thick skulls. I'm the very last person to have wanted Fletcher dead." For a fleeting moment, emotion cut through her expression; she swallowed and banished it, then more quietly repeated, "It wasn't me."

Barnaby straightened. "You said Riggs would have you—has he been pursuing you?"

Kitty shrugged. "Just the usual—nothing I couldn't handle. I had to butter him up to learn what Fletcher needed to know about the safe and the family and Riggs took that as encouragement, so I've been treading a little carefully where he's concerned."

Barnaby ran his mind over their questions and her answers thus far, then asked, "You told us of the letter you got from Fletcher informing you that he was coming back." He caught Kitty's gaze. "When you got it, what did you *think* was behind it? What did you think was Fletcher's new plan?"

Kitty grimaced and slowly shook her head. "Honestly? I had no idea.

Knowing Fletcher, even given what was written in the letter—he was always careful what he put in writing—it could simply have been that something had gone wrong and he was coming to fetch me away. I packed my bag just in case, but..." Kitty shut her lips and said nothing more.

Barnaby studied her, then looked at Stokes. He couldn't decide if she was telling the truth or was simply that good an actress.

From the frustrated expression in his eyes, Stokes couldn't either.

In this case, jealousy had seemed the obvious motive to account for the passion behind the murder, but if not that...where did that leave them?

Barnaby looked back at Kitty. "Why did you leave this morning?"

Her gaze lowering to the desktop, Kitty lightly shrugged. "I'd had enough of this place. I had no reason to stay and you've taken Fletcher's body to town. I wanted to see about giving him a decent burial—we've got enough put away for that."

Someone rapped on the door.

At Stokes's terse "Yes," Jones looked in.

"Mr. Culver and Miss Finsbury heard as how we'd caught Miss Mallard waiting for the coach and that she's our prime suspect. They say they have something to show you that proves it couldn't have been a woman did for Fletcher."

Stokes arched his brows. "Indeed?" After a second, he looked at Kitty. "I suggest it would be in your best interests for you to remain here while Adair and I check this evidence, which, according to Culver and Miss Finsbury, will prove your innocence."

Sitting back, Kitty waved them to the door. "By all means. I didn't kill Fletcher and the sooner you believe that the better off I'll be—and perhaps, then, you can find the real murderer."

Stokes rose and, with Barnaby on his heels, headed for the door. Somewhat to Barnaby's surprise, Stokes paused on the threshold and looked back at his constable who was still standing guard behind Kitty's chair. "Phipps."

When the constable looked around, Stokes tipped his head toward the corridor.

Stokes stepped through the door, Barnaby followed, and Phipps brought up the rear, closing the door behind him. Duffet was still standing beside the door. Glancing down the corridor, Barnaby saw Jones waiting with Frederick Culver and Gwendolyn Finsbury where the corridor debouched into the front hall.

Stokes looked at Duffet. "I want you to stay on guard here and make sure Miss Mallard doesn't leave the room, no matter what excuse she gives. We won't be long." Looking at Phipps, Stokes's expression hardened. "I want you outside the house. Find someplace to lurk where you can't be seen from the office windows, but from where you'll see if Miss Mallard tries to escape." Stokes met Barnaby's eyes. "She ran this morning—let's see if, presented with the opportunity, she runs again."

Barnaby arched his brows but nodded. "If, despite all, she does run again, then she's definitely not innocent. She might not have done the deed but if she's anxious enough to bolt, she had something to do with Fletcher's demise."

"Right." His expression grim, Stokes looked down the corridor. "Now let's see what these two have found."

Ten minutes later, Barnaby stood alongside Stokes in an outbuilding beyond the shrubbery and stared at the small mountain of heavy farming equipment that had been lifted aside to gain access to the foot-trap.

As the outline the foot-trap had left in the dust was plain to see, the obvious conclusion was impossible to deny.

When Stokes remained silent, Barnaby stated it aloud. "No woman acting alone could have gained access to the trap."

Culver, standing to one side with Gwendolyn Finsbury and the estate's old gardener, shifted. "That's not all." When Barnaby and Stokes glanced his way, Culver went on, "Penman here says that there's a narrow trail through the wood that leads to the path from the village. I've been wondering how we—Gwen and I—could have missed the murderer returning to the house, but if he knew about the trap and got it from here, he almost certainly knew about the trail and he wouldn't have needed to risk crossing the side lawn and possibly running into some of the guests."

Stokes nodded grimly. "Indeed." He swung toward the door.

"But there's more." When Stokes halted, Culver continued, "We looked in the croquet shed and Agnes's hoop-hammer—actually a long-handled sledgehammer very like the one used on Mitchell—is still in there. It wasn't the murder weapon."

Stokes stared at him with something akin to disbelief.

Culver hurriedly added, "But the long-handled sledgehammer that's part of the estate's tools and that should be hanging on a rack in the barn is missing."

Stokes shifted his gaze to the gardener. "Who among the household would have known that there was a sledgehammer kept in the barn?"

The gardener primmed his lips, but eventually consented to answer. "Only the staff. I can imagine his lordship might've known we'd have a trap hidden in the outbuildings somewhere, but he wouldn't have known where, not without a lot of searching, and no way can I imagine he'd have known that we had another sledgehammer, much less where it was kept. We only use it for the fences and we haven't done them in a couple of years."

Gwendolyn Finsbury put in, "The rack where the tools hang can't be seen from the barn door—you have to go all the way inside, almost to the rear wall, before you see it."

Barnaby glanced at Stokes, who almost imperceptibly shook his head.

Face set, Stokes looked at Culver, Miss Finsbury, and the gardener. He nodded. "Thank you. I don't yet know what this means—how it will play out—but your help has been crucial." With a swift glance at Barnaby, he continued, "Now if you'll excuse us? Oh, and if you would ensure this building is locked and the key given to..." Stokes looked at Miss Finsbury. "Perhaps for the moment, miss, you would agree to hold the key. Just until we sort this out."

Gwendolyn Finsbury nodded. "Yes, of course."

Alongside Stokes, Barnaby strode swiftly back toward the house. "Who the devil was it? A man, obviously, but was he acting with Kitty, as her accomplice, or is she not involved at all and the murderer was after Fletcher for some entirely different reason?"

"Regardless," Stokes said, and the tenor of his voice suggested anticipation was riding high, "you heard the gardener. It had to be one of the staff. Moreover, one of the staff who has been here for long enough to have had the time to stumble on the trap, the trail, and the sledgehammer."

"Ah—yes." Barnaby felt his own excitement building; they were close, so close. "The gardener put his finger on it—whoever the murderer was, he had to have known the trap was there. He could only have learned the evening before that Fletcher—Mitchell—was planning to return. And while the staff's time is not completely accounted for, none of them had enough *unaccounted* time to have spent hours searching to discover something with which to trap Fletcher."

"Exactly." Stokes led the way up the front steps. Closing his hand on the doorknob, he paused. Then he grimaced and met Barnaby's eyes. "Unfortunately, despite the gardener's assertions, this brings Lord Finsbury back into contention."

Barnaby met Stokes's gaze, then pulled a face. "Damn. You're right. We keep going around and around with Finsbury."

"It's the motive we're lacking, at least in his case. If he killed Fletcher-Mitchell to retrieve the diamonds, why did he leave them in Fletcher's pocket and then look so shocked when Duffet returned them to him?" Stokes shook his head.

Barnaby raised his hands in a helpless gesture. "And we *still* don't know why Fletcher was bringing them back. I keep thinking that's the key —the reason Fletcher returned—but the diamonds were left on his body, so how can that be?"

"Don't ask me." Stokes sighed and opened the door. "Let's go and see if Kitty has tried to do a flit, or if she's been sitting innocently in the office all the time we've been gone."

Barnaby's mind flashed back to Kitty as he'd last seen her, in the last minutes before they'd left the office...

Instead of following Stokes, he stood rooted to the spot. "Wait—wait!"

"What now?" Stokes reappeared in the doorway through which he'd already gone.

Barnaby held up a hand. "I just remembered...all the questions we put to Kitty—she looked at us when she answered. Every time. Until the last question I asked her."

Stokes blinked. After a moment, he said, "Why she left this morning."

His gaze distant, remembering the scene, Barnaby nodded. "Yes. When she answered that question, she looked down at the desk." He refocused on Stokes. "She didn't meet our eyes."

Stokes thumped his fist on the door frame. "That was a lie." Turning, he made for the corridor to the estate office.

Barnaby followed close behind. "Not only was it a lie—it was her *only* lie."

"Someone tipped her off," Stokes growled, striding faster.

"Indeed," Barnaby replied, keeping pace. "So the only question now is who—and if we're still looking for the motive for Fletcher's murder, it'll probably be the why."

Gaining the corridor leading to the office with Barnaby at his back, Stokes saw Duffet standing outside the office door, but instead of standing with his back to the panels, appropriately on guard, the constable was facing the door, head tilted as if listening to something inside.

Stokes slowed. Barnaby did the same. Their feet made little sound on the corridor runner as they drew nearer.

Duffet sensed their presence and glanced their way. His expression was already worried before he saw them.

"What is it?" Stokes whispered. Then he, too, heard the voices coming from the office, the words muffled by the thick oak panels. "Who is it?" he amended. When the hapless Duffet didn't immediately answer, Stokes pinned him with his gaze and baldly asked, "Who did you let in there?"

"The butler, sir. Riggs." Duffet had the sense to whisper his reply. "He came along with a cup of tea. You said not to let her out, but I didn't see any harm in him taking her a cup of tea."

Stokes glanced at Barnaby—who returned the look with interest.

Crash!

The sound came from within the office.

It was instantly followed by a strangled cry.

Opening the door, Stokes rushed inside; Barnaby was on his heels.

Both paused for an instant, taking in the scene—Riggs and Kitty on the other side of the desk, struggling before the window, Riggs with his hands locked about Kitty's neck, strangling the life out of her—then Stokes went one way, Barnaby the other.

Rounding the desk, Barnaby grabbed Riggs's shoulders and tried to haul him off, but Riggs, his features contorted, his eyes wild and foam flecking his lips, was intent on crushing Kitty's throat.

Stokes aimed a fist over Kitty's shoulder.

Bone crunched. Riggs jerked, his head snapping back.

Stokes pried Riggs's fingers from Kitty's neck and swung her away, putting her behind him and facing Riggs himself.

Riggs roared and, dragging Barnaby with him, went after Kitty—entirely ignoring Stokes who stood directly in his way. "*Whore*! *Jezebel*! What do you mean you're going back to London?" His face beet-red, Riggs shook with the violence of his feelings; his eyes, locked on Kitty's face, burned. "I *killed* that bounder for your sake, so you could stay here with me—but you're leaving? Oh, no. No, no, *no!*" A vicious expression transforming his face, Riggs strained to reach Kitty. "You're not leaving me. I'll kill you first!"

Boots thundered in the corridor. Phipps and Jones burst into the room, took stock in one glance, and plunged into action.

Stokes all but lifted Kitty aside. With one boot, he pushed a chair to the side of the room and sat her down. "Stay there."

The order was superfluous. Kitty was still gasping and wheezing.

Turning, Stokes saw that between them, Barnaby, Phipps, and Jones had managed to restrain the raging Riggs. He still hadn't quieted but continued to spew invectives and epithets, all directed at Kitty. His earlier "whore" and "Jezebel" were the least objectionable.

Phipps produced a piece of rope and deftly tied Riggs's wrists.

Stokes waved at the door. "Take him away—preferably outside. Both of you stay with him."

"Aye, sir." Phipps nodded and, with Jones, half marched, half lifted Riggs out of the room.

Riggs didn't stop yelling, but his threats gradually faded until finally relative silence returned.

Stokes looked at Barnaby. "Well, that's the murderer caught."

"True." Barnaby was studying Kitty. "But as I see it, we're still not entirely clear as to his motive."

Following Barnaby's gaze, Stokes caught his drift. Riggs might have been the murderer, but had Kitty put him up to it? Had she known of Riggs' intention and, possibly, encouraged him?

Barnaby drew the other chair around and sat facing Kitty.

Stokes propped himself against the corner of the desk, folded his arms, and watched Kitty's face.

"Kitty," Barnaby said, his voice even and unthreatening. "You need to tell us what that was all about."

Kitty's face was parchment pale, her eyes huge. She was still in shock —actress that she was, this might well be the best chance they would have to extract the unvarnished truth.

Her gaze unfocused, Kitty swallowed, and winced.

Stokes glanced at the door and saw Duffet, round-eyed, peering in. "Fetch her another cup of tea. And tell the cook to put some honey in it."

Duffet vanished.

Kitty vaguely nodded her thanks. She moistened her lips. "I didn't realize…" The words were a thread of sound. Drawing in a deeper breath, one hand rising to her bruised throat, she went on, "I told you that I had to encourage Riggs a trifle to get him to tell me what we—Fletcher and I— needed to know. Afterward, he—Riggs—was…attentive. I said it wasn't anything I couldn't handle, and it wasn't, but there was an *intensity* about his regard that was…unsettling. Then when Fletcher arrived, Riggs saw the pair of us meeting in the shrubbery. I played it off, and so did Fletcher, as just a flirting exchange, but from then on Riggs watched me like a hawk. I had to be extra careful slipping away to meet Fletcher—I made sure Riggs was busy in the house before I did. Then Fletcher left— meaning that as Mitchell he was thrown out—and Riggs…relaxed. I thought with Fletcher gone, I would have no more trouble."

Dragging in a shuddering breath, Kitty paused. Her expression was all contrition and sorrow; tears glimmered in her eyes.

If this was an act, Barnaby thought, it was the performance of her life.

Her voice little more than a whisper, Kitty went on, "Then Fletcher's letter arrived. I didn't realize until later that, of course, Riggs receives the mail. He brought my letter to me. I took it and tucked it into my pocket and went on with my work. He waited for a minute, then left. I didn't open the letter until I was alone in my room, and I burnt it after I'd read it." Kitty shivered. "But, of course, Riggs also delivered Fletcher's other letter to Miss Finsbury. I can't be sure, but I suspect that Fletcher hadn't thought and his handwriting was the same on both letters. Riggs guessed —well, knew—that the letter I'd received came from, as he thought, Mitchell."

Kitty paused to pass her tongue over her lips. "I told you that, on the night before Fletcher returned, I packed my bag just in case his new plan meant I had to leave with him. Riggs came to my door while I was pack- ing. I didn't let him in—he said he wanted to talk, and I said I was tired and I would see him the next day. But the bag was open on the bed—he saw it over my shoulder. I know he looked, then he looked back at my face, but he said nothing and I told him good night and shut the door."

She drew in an even more shaky breath, and when she spoke, her voice quavered. "I gathered"—she tipped her head toward the space before the window—"that Riggs believed that Fletcher had charmed me into running away with him. I...suppose that's why he decided to kill Fletcher before he reached the house." She shook her head. "I don't know."

After a moment, Barnaby asked, his voice calm, almost gentle, "I asked earlier why you'd left this morning. I don't think you would have planned to go, so...."

Kitty's breath caught. She glanced at Stokes. "I wasn't intending to leave, not until you'd found who'd murdered Fletcher." Her voice steadied; her features firmed. "I wanted to know who had killed him. But then this morning Riggs came rushing up and told me you'd arrived, and that he'd heard you tell Lord Finsbury that you were convinced that I'd killed Fletcher—he had the name, Fletcher, so I knew you'd learned that much and that Riggs was speaking the truth. He insisted that I had to leave. I didn't know what to do. Riggs all but bundled me out of the house. He told me to go to a nearby barn and wait for him there, that it would be all right—that he would sort it all out."

Meeting Barnaby's eyes, Kitty shook her head. "I have no idea what he meant by that, but I didn't wait to find out. I left via the path—the barn is a little way off it—but instead of going there, I went on to the village, to the coaching inn, and bought a ticket back to London." She looked at Stokes. "That's where your men found me."

Stokes nodded. He glanced at Barnaby, but he, too, had no more questions.

Kitty stared across the room, then her face crumpled. "I tried to let Riggs down gently—it should have worked. It has in the past...." A second ticked by, then she bowed her head, covering her face with her hands. "Oh, my God—he killed Fletcher because of *me*."

Kitty's shoulders shook as she wept.

Stokes exchanged an uneasy glance with Barnaby.

Then a stir at the door heralded Mrs. Bateman with a tray.

The housekeeper took in the scene, then bustled forward. "There, there, dear." Setting the tray on the desk, the older woman shooed Barnaby aside and swooped in and took the weeping Kitty into her arms. "It'll be all right—you'll see."

Leaving Mrs. Bateman to comfort Kitty, Barnaby beat a hasty retreat, unsurprised to find Stokes close behind him.

Quietly shutting the door, Stokes met his gaze. "I believe that gives us our motive."

Barnaby nodded. "I sincerely doubt that that was an act. She and Fletcher were a true team."

The word was one their wives—Penelope especially—were wont to use.

"But," Barnaby said, "we're still left with one burning question unanswered."

Stokes frowned. "What question?"

"Why did Fletcher return to the house?" Barnaby paused, then said, "I need to listen to my wife more often." He met Stokes's gaze. "She instructed me to get a look at the Finsbury diamonds, and I believe in her condition I should do all I can to humor her." He tipped his head. "Coming?"

"If you think that's going to answer our burning question"—Stokes waved him on—"lead the way."

CHAPTER 7

*B*arnaby knocked on the door of Lord Finsbury's study.

Hearing a gruff, "Come," he opened the door and went in.

Lord Finsbury was sitting behind his desk. He'd been staring out of the window, but now swiveled to face them. Anxiety rode his features; uncertainty filled his face. "I heard the commotion. What's happened?"

The study was in a separate wing from the estate office; his lordship would have been able to hear the noise, but wouldn't have been able to discern who was involved.

Stokes had followed Barnaby into the room. At a glance from Barnaby, Stokes replied, "We've apprehended the murderer, my lord. It was Riggs, your butler."

"*Riggs?*" Incredulity banished anxiety; Lord Finsbury goggled. "Great heavens! What possible reason could Riggs have had for attacking Mitchell—that is, this Fletcher person?"

"As to that," Stokes said, "we believe the reason was the parlormaid, Kitty Mallard. As we mentioned earlier, she was Fletcher's lover and accomplice, introduced into the household to collect the necessary information for Fletcher's scheme, but all Riggs saw was a maid he wanted being seduced by the charms of a gentleman-rake. He killed Mitchell-Fletcher out of jealousy, because he saw Fletcher as a successful rival for Kitty's affections."

Stokes paused, then added, "We have no reason to suppose that Kitty was involved, other than inadvertently—she did not appreciate the danger

Riggs, being the sort of obsessively possessive man he is, posed to her and Fletcher."

Clasping his hands before him, Lord Finsbury stared at them for several moments, then the brittle tension that had held him eased. "So." He raised his gaze to Stokes's face. "It's over, then."

Stokes glanced at Barnaby.

"In the main." Barnaby met Lord Finsbury's gaze. "But there's one point we have yet to resolve. To do so, we need to examine the necklace —the Finsbury diamonds."

Lord Finsbury had long ago lost the ability to hide his emotions; deep-seated reluctance colored his features. He regarded Barnaby steadily, resistance holding firm, but then his shoulders lowered and, slowly, he nodded. Pushing back from the desk, he rose. "Yes, I suppose you do."

His tone held threads of regret and re-emerging anxiety.

Crossing to the large portrait hanging on the side wall, his lordship swung the picture aside, revealing a large wall safe.

Barnaby noted that it was an older model from a popular maker; child's play for any decent cracksman—or a dexterous amateur like Fletcher.

After spinning the large dial, then opening the heavy door, Lord Finsbury reached inside. He hesitated for a moment, then, his posture suggesting he was girding his loins, he lifted a black velvet jewelry case and, turning, returned to the desk.

Halting behind it, Lord Finsbury opened the case, looked down at the contents for several seconds, then, raising his head, he held out the open case to Barnaby. "These are the Finsbury diamonds."

The introduction was hardly necessary; the diamonds, dozens of square stones each as large as the nail on Barnaby's little finger, plus several even larger round ones, all set in a heavy but simple setting, were every bit as fabulous as their reputation painted them. Even in the relatively poor light in the study, the diamonds blazed.

Barnaby lifted the necklace from its bed. He held it up before his face, the stones a cascade of brilliant white fire, sparking and flashing as he turned his fingers.

He didn't need to look too closely; the weight of the necklace told him all he needed to know.

Barnaby glanced at Stokes. His stoic friend was staring at the glittering stones as if he'd never beheld such bounty.

Hiding a smile, Barnaby returned the necklace to the case, then closed the case and held it out to Lord Finsbury. "Thank you."

Somewhat hesitantly, his lordship took back the case. A frown in his eyes, he searched Barnaby's face...then, softly, he sighed. "You know they're paste."

Barnaby inclined his head, his gaze steady on Lord Finsbury's. "But I can't see that anyone else needs to know."

The relief that swept his lordship was dramatic; for a moment, he hardly dared believe his ears, then he did, and his demeanor, his entire stance, changed, lightening, as if he'd just sloughed off a massive weight. His movements less stiff than before, he inclined his head to Barnaby. "Thank you."

"One last question." Stokes had quickly readjusted his assumptions. He nodded at the black velvet case. "When were the real gems replaced?"

Lord Finsbury looked down at the case. "In my father's day."

Barnaby remarked, "That's why the necklace is so rarely seen in public." Another mystery solved.

Lord Finsbury nodded. "The events at which it appears have to be chosen carefully—in an old-fashioned ballroom under candlelight, the substitution is effectively impossible to detect, not unless one examines the stones carefully, and even then one would need a good eye and a jeweler's loupe. But with improved lighting..." He paused, then sighed. "I fear that, at some point in the near future, the Finsbury diamonds are going to be tragically lost."

Stokes looked at Barnaby. "So when Fletcher realized the diamonds were fake, he came back to try another tack."

Lord Finsbury, not realizing the comment was not directed at him, shook his head. "I have no notion, Inspector. I didn't speak with the man again. However, you can now understand the depths of my shock when Duffet returned the diamonds to me. I had had no idea they'd been taken, and although Mitchell—Fletcher—was dead, I had no way of knowing if he'd learned our family secret, and if he had told anyone else."

Stokes had been studying his lordship; now he nodded. "Thank you, sir." Stokes glanced at Barnaby. "I believe that will be all." When Barnaby nodded in agreement, Stokes continued, "We have all the testimony we require. We'll be relieving you of our company shortly, and taking Riggs and Miss Mallard with us."

Lord Finsbury frowned. "As to that, Inspector, Mr. Adair, I wonder if I might make a request?"

When both Stokes and Barnaby raised their brows in invitation, Lord Finsbury elaborated, "The guests, and Agnes and Gwen, and Frederick, and the staff, too—they'll all want some explanation and, I fear, dealing with such situations is not my forte. I wondered if you would consent to have a quick word—perhaps in the drawing room once we've gathered everyone together?"

Stokes exchanged a glance with Barnaby. "I think we could manage that."

Barnaby grinned. "Why not? Everyone loves a good denouement."

Leaving Lord Finsbury to gather his household, Stokes and Barnaby stepped out onto the front porch. There they found Duffet standing guard by the front door; Stokes sent him to fetch Kitty Mallard. "Tell her we'll need her at the Yard to give a full statement. I doubt she'll argue."

Duffet saluted and left.

Barnaby softly snorted. "I suspect Kitty will be only too grateful for a reason to leave."

"Hmm." Stokes looked across the forecourt to where Phipps, Jones, and the Yard driver were gathered by the coach, which had been drawn to the side of the gravel drive. A few yards away, Riggs sat cross-legged on the lawn. His arms now tied behind his back, he was rocking back and forth and talking aloud, quite intently, to someone who wasn't there.

"Do you think he'll stand trial?" Barnaby asked.

"I'm not sure." Stokes shook his head. "Even to the end, he seemed rational enough, but...who knows when it comes to the corruption of men's minds."

A moment passed, then Stokes stirred. "Speaking of corruption of trains of thought, those diamonds have dogged our steps at every turn, yet although we had the chance, we didn't bother examining them."

"Indeed." Barnaby paused, then continued, "Yet if we had..."

"Precisely." Stokes nodded. "Lord Finsbury would have gone straight to the top of our list of suspects and, most likely, stayed there. We wouldn't have kept blundering around searching for clues—his lordship would have had opportunity, means, and one hell of a motive. Even the Chief Commissioner would have pressed ahead with the case. And we would have been wrong."

After a moment, Barnaby offered, "The Finsbury diamonds might be fake, but, rather than being cursed, perhaps they're blessed."

"His lordship still needs funds," Stokes said.

"True," Barnaby allowed. "But if the looks exchanged between Miss Finsbury and Culver are any guide, his lordship will be hearing wedding bells soon enough, and, while I was inquiring after the non-existent Mitchell, I heard a whisper or two about Culver, who is anything but non-existent. The word is that he returned from Africa a very wealthy man, but has chosen to play his cards close to his chest—the assumption being that he doesn't want to be hounded by the matchmakers."

"Wise man—especially as it seems he's had his match in his sights all along."

"Indeed." Barnaby looked across at Riggs. "Oddly enough, I think it must have been Culver who, entirely innocently, was behind Fletcher returning here. The instant Fletcher learned that the necklace was paste, his mind would have turned to blackmail, but he knew Lord Finsbury had no wealth to speak of—the fake diamonds were testament enough to that. But Culver? Culver wanted to marry Gwen. Fletcher would have immediately asked around and he would have heard the same whispers about Culver that I did. So Fletcher sent his letter to Gwen, asking to meet her, but it was Culver he intended to speak with—after their earlier contretemps, Fletcher knew Culver would be by Gwen's side." Barnaby paused, then, his tone hardening, he concluded, "Fletcher was planning to use Gwen's family's standing, her happiness, to blackmail Culver."

A moment ticked past, then Stokes said, "Culver would have paid."

"Yes, he would have. Most likely for the rest of Fletcher's and Kitty's lives." Barnaby stirred. "Which is why Fletcher considered his revised plan to be even better than stealing the diamonds."

After a moment, Stokes murmured, "Rather than being blessed, perhaps fake diamonds bring death to those who steal them."

Barnaby's lips eased. He tipped his head. "Perhaps. There would be a certain appropriateness in that."

The door opened and Duffet looked out. "His lordship says as they're ready for you, sir."

Meeting Barnaby's eyes, Stokes arched his brows. "Ready for our performance?"

Barnaby grinned and waved him on. "After you."

~

That was, in fact, how they tackled their denouement. They entered the drawing room to discover that everyone, not only the guests and family, but every member of the staff barring only Riggs and Kitty, were gathered to hear their report.

Lord Finsbury briefly introduced them, then Stokes took the floor and gave a concise account of what was now known to be the sequence of events, commencing with Fletcher's scheme to steal the diamonds, then explaining Kitty's part in the plan and Riggs's unanticipated jealousy over her undeclared attachment to Mitchell-Fletcher, which had led to Riggs laying the foot-trap on the path and beating Fletcher to death.

Stokes tied all the physical evidence neatly into his tale, and before anyone could question why Fletcher had returned to the house with the diamonds in his pocket, Barnaby stepped in. "Everything we now know indicates that Fletcher had had a change of heart." He smiled easily at all the attentive faces. "We believe he intended to return the necklace to the family."

Both statements were entirely true.

Stokes retook the stage to conclude, "While the violent murder of Gordon Fletcher, known to you as Peter Mitchell, has undoubtedly been a trial to you all, we are confident we have apprehended all those involved, and that none of those remaining at Finsbury Court had anything whatever to do with the crime." He glanced at Lord Finsbury. "On behalf of the Chief Commissioner, I would like to thank his lordship for his support and assistance in allowing us to deal with this matter expeditiously, and also to extend special thanks to Mr. Culver and Miss Finsbury for their efforts in uncovering the source of what were, in effect, the murder weapons." Stokes favored the company with a half-bow. "Thank you all for your assistance."

As Stokes stepped back, Barnaby swept the company with a smile. "And might I tender our hopes that the rest of the house party passes with a little less excitement?"

Laughter rippled through the assembly. People smiled and turned to speak to each other.

Lord Finsbury shook Barnaby's, then Stokes's hand. "Thank you both. That will silence the whisperers."

"Indeed." Agnes Finsbury had come up, Gwendolyn and Frederick in her wake. Agnes shook Barnaby's hand, then, without a blink, extended her hand to Stokes. "I can't thank you enough, Inspector—that was very well done. While there will certainly be talk about this incident—the murder at the house party at Finsbury Court—rather than being scandalized, the tone of such comments will now be about the drama and excitement our guests were privileged to witness."

Stokes struggled to hide a cynical smile. "If you say so, ma'am."

"Oh, I know so, sir." With a pat on Stokes's arm, Agnes moved on.

Somewhat to Stokes's surprise, if not Barnaby's, many of the guests milled around, wanting to shake their hands and compliment them on a job well done.

They'd expected to leave immediately, but the minutes ticked on.

Faint sounds came from outside, then a thunderous knocking on the door shocked everyone into silence.

Everyone waited, then, with a startled yelp, Percy, the footman, now elevated to butler, remembered the duty that was now his and rushed out to open the front door.

A deep voice sounded briefly in the hall; a prickle of awareness tickled Barnaby's nape.

Then heavy footsteps approached. A second later, Conner, Barnaby's groom, appeared in the doorway. The usually imperturbable man looked disheveled and wild. Conner's gaze swept the gathering and landed on Barnaby. "Sir! It's the mistress!" Suddenly becoming aware of the interested crowd, Conner swallowed the words he'd been about to say and substituted, "You have to come now."

Barnaby's world stopped turning; the summons could mean only one thing.

Stokes slapped him on the back. "Go! I'll take care of all here."

Eyes round, Conner said, "I've brought the curricle."

Barnaby managed a nod. To Lord Finsbury, he said, "I have to go."

Even those words were an effort; his heart had leapt and lodged high in his throat.

With a general nod to the company—he was barely aware of them now—Barnaby made for the doorway. Waving Conner back, he strode quickly out of the room. Reaching the front hall, he broke into a run.

It was one thing to know that your wife was going to have a baby, and quite another to discover that she was actually having it.

Several hours later, Barnaby paced before the fireplace in his library, a glass of brandy clutched in one hand, and tried to think of something

—*anything*—other than the fear that, entirely unexpectedly, had him in a viselike grip.

He'd driven back to town like a madman. Leaving his curricle slewed in the street, he'd rushed into the house and raced up the stairs—only to be met at the door of the bedroom Penelope had chosen as her accouchement chamber by a wall of disapproving females.

His mother, Aurelia, Countess of Cothelstone, together with Penelope's mother, Minerva, Dowager Viscountess of Calverton, had smiled somewhat patronizingly on him and gently, but firmly, shooed him away.

Penelope's sisters—Emily, Anne, and Portia—had ignored him entirely.

He hadn't even managed to get a clear glimpse of the small but bloated figure lying in the bed.

His wife. And for the first time in his life he was truly terrified that he might lose her.

Women—even ladies—died in childbirth every day.

What if Penelope died?

If she was close to death, would they tell him?

Or would he be left down here in ignorance while she passed away without him there?

Helpless. He truly was helpless to save her.

About him, their staff crept about, as unnerved as he.

Eventually, he'd had the bright idea of sending Mostyn up to inquire whether the doctor—Simmonds from Harley Street—should be summoned.

The answer had been "No."

Apparently it was too early.

Which suggested that there were many more hours of the torture of not knowing ahead of him.

After delivering the news, Mostyn had quietly retreated. Barnaby had half a mind to join the staff in the kitchen—if he remained here alone, by the time anything happened and he was told whatever news there was, he would be three sheets to the wind and in no state to cope.

A sharp glance at the brandy decanter revealed that Mostyn must have filled it to the brim in anticipation of his need.

Barnaby grunted, turned, and paced back across the hearth.

The front door bell rang.

Halting, Barnaby listened. Had the harridans upstairs relented and sent for the doctor after all?

But then he heard footsteps heading for the library, a heavy, deliberate tread he recognized.

The door opened and his father entered. Locating Barnaby, the earl smiled, closed the door, and came forward. He pointed at Barnaby's glass. "You can give me one of those."

Moving to oblige, Barnaby glanced at his father. "What are you doing here?"

The earl subsided into one of the pair of armchairs before the hearth. "I was at the Yard when Stokes brought in his prisoner. He gave us the bare outline—enough to ease the Chief Commissioner's mind. But as for the rest—ah, thank you." The earl accepted the glass Barnaby handed him and took an appreciative sip. "Where was I? Oh, yes—Stokes mentioned that you had rushed off as Penelope's time had come, so being an old hand at suffering through the hours of waiting, I thought I'd come here and get the full details of the case from you—and, in so doing, keep you from going insane."

Looking into his father's cheery face, into his understanding eyes, Barnaby couldn't help but smile, however wanly, in reply. "Yes, well—I admit it's wearying in a way I hadn't foreseen."

"Precisely." The earl waved Barnaby to the other chair. "So do as I say, and sit and tell me everything that happened with this case. Trust me"—a twinkle in his eye, the earl met Barnaby's gaze—"the first time is almost always hellishly long—you've got hours more to endure."

With a resigned sigh, Barnaby sat, focused his mind on the events at Finsbury Court, and proceeded to tell his father all.

Dinner that evening at Finsbury Court was a relaxed and truly pleasant affair. Everyone was pleased with the outcome of the investigation. As Agnes had foretold, all the guests were delighted to have had the experience of watching a murder investigation unfold; when they returned to their separate spheres, their observations would make them interesting for weeks, if not months.

Relief was the principal emotion felt by the family, and that on so many counts. As for the staff, despite having been their leader for a decade and more, Riggs had had no real friends; on inquiring, Agnes had discovered that he had never been popular, merely tolerated. His loss was not felt deeply.

Eventually, the ladies rose from the table and left the gentlemen to pass the port. The gentlemen did, but didn't linger, rejoining the ladies in good time. This was the last night of the house party; tomorrow, everyone would return to their homes. For once, the gentlemen joined the ladies in their groups, the better to share the memories.

Frederick had eyes only for Gwen. He made his way to where she stood beside Harriet and Algernon. After greeting the others, under cover of their conversation Frederick leaned closer to Gwen and murmured, "I've asked your father for an interview. He agreed and has gone ahead to his study. I would like you, and Agnes, too, to be present." He met Gwen's widening eyes. "Will you come?"

Her smile lit his world. "Of course." Setting her hand on his arm, she turned and excused them. Leaving Harriet and Algernon deep in their own exchanges, Gwen steered Frederick to where Agnes sat beside Mrs. Shepherd and Mrs. Pace.

With a quick word, Gwen extracted Agnes and Frederick escorted both ladies from the room.

In such a small party, their departure would be noted and everyone would, of course, guess the cause. An unexpected betrothal would set the seal on this house party being declared an unmitigated success.

Ushering Agnes and Gwen into his lordship's study, Frederick felt an unaccustomed flutter afflict his usually rock-steady nerves. This was it— the moment he'd worked toward for more years than he wished to count. And quite aside from his request, he would have to make a confession.

Worse, as he saw Agnes and Gwen to the chairs before his lordship's desk, Frederick realized that his confession would have to come first, before he could ask Gwen for her answer.

"Well, my boy." Lord Finsbury looked at Frederick as he straightened, standing beside Gwen's chair.

To Frederick's eyes, Lord Finsbury did not appear to be as resistant toward him as he had been, yet neither did his lordship appear encouraging. Resigned was nearer the mark.

Drawing in a breath and feeling his lungs constrict, Frederick resisted the urge to clear his throat and simply stated, "My lord, I wish to ask for your permission to pay my addresses to Gwen. I would very much like to ask her to be my wife."

Gwen turned her head and smiled radiantly up at him. Reaching out, she closed her fingers about his hand.

Frederick looked down into her beloved face. "But before we go any further, I have a confession of sorts to make. Not just to Gwen"—he shifted his gaze to Agnes—"but to Agnes, too." When both ladies tilted their heads in almost identical fashion and looked inquiringly at him, he girded his loins and went on, "I know I've led you both to believe that I am, at best, barely well-to-do. That I'm not wealthy."

Glancing across the desk at Lord Finsbury, who was now frowning, Frederick said, "With all due respect, my lord, I knew you were keen on Gwen marrying a wealthy man, but"—he looked at Gwen and met her eyes—"I didn't want her marrying me for such a reason. I wanted her to marry me...because she wished to marry me."

"And I do." Gwen uttered the words with simple honesty and a great deal of determination. She looked at her father.

Who was now staring at Frederick and looking utterly perplexed.

"Are you saying," Lord Finsbury said, "that you *are* wealthy? That you're not *not wealthy*?"

"Yes." Frederick nodded. "Precisely." He glanced at Agnes, then looked back at Lord Finsbury. "I believe I'm now referred to as a very warm man."

Lord Finsbury sat back, faint shock and rather more definite respect dawning in his face. "You managed it. Your father always told me you would make your mark in Africa, but so many have tried and not even made it back...I really didn't think you would succeed."

Frederick managed a smile. "But I did." He glanced at Agnes, whose eyes were shining, then he looked at Gwen. He shifted his fingers and closed them about hers. "I'm sorry for the deception, but I needed to know that you felt for me as I do for you."

Gwen's smile was all delight. "I understand. And to my mind, you have nothing of any moment to apologize for."

Frederick drank in her absolution and the blatant love in her eyes. He forced himself to look away, to look at Lord Finsbury. "As I've already told Gwen, I've reacquired the land my family used to own, and, of course, I inherited the house. The estate is now in my hands, unencumbered, and it's my intention to make our home there."

Agnes heaved a gusty sigh. "That's wonderful! It's exactly what your mothers both hoped for."

Frederick kept his gaze locked on Lord Finsbury. "Sir?"

Smiling more broadly, his lordship waved expansively. "Of course, you have my permission, my boy—and I apologize for not having sufficient faith in you."

Inclining his head, Frederick swallowed the revelation that it was his attachment to Gwen—his love for her—that had driven him and seen him through…to now. He looked into her eyes and the rest of the world faded. "What say you, Gwen?" The most important answer of all—the only one that mattered.

Gwen looked at him with her heart in her eyes. "Yes—I forgive you. Yes—I will marry you. And yes—I adore you and will until I die."

Frederick raised her hand to his lips and pressed an ardent kiss to her fingers. "And I will love you come hell or high water, until my dying day."

The doctor had finally been sent for. Simmonds, a short, slightly portly practitioner renowned for his no-nonsense manner, had duly arrived; he had merely nodded to Barnaby, waiting, eaten with anxiety, in the front hall, then Simonds had walked past and had ascended the stairs.

That had been two hours ago. It was now nearly midnight and Barnaby wasn't sure his nerves would hold up for much longer.

Despite his father's presence, he'd resumed his pacing; ineffective though the activity was, at least he was moving.

The tension had steadily escalated over the past hour; he felt it as a palpable weight bearing down on his shoulders.

Barnaby halted. The need to rush upstairs and demand to be told what was going on was close to overpowering—

A lusty cry resounded through the house.

Stunned, Barnaby looked up—toward where the sound had come from.

His father, who had been calmly reading the day's news sheets, looked up and smiled. "Ah—there we are." Setting the news sheets aside, the earl got to his feet and clapped his son on the shoulder. "Congratulations, my boy—you're a father now."

Still stunned, Barnaby absentmindedly allowed the earl to wring his hand…*he was a father*.

He had a child.

Emotion of a sort he'd never experienced crashed over him, all but drowning his faculties, his wits, with its power.

After a moment, he swallowed and managed to croak, "What now?" He blinked and looked at his father. "Can I go up, do you think?"

Smiling, the earl shook his head. "Not yet. We still have to wait."

A full half an hour later, they heard heavy footsteps descending the stairs.

Barnaby reached the front hall as Simmonds, beaming genially, stepped off the last tread. After nodding to Mostyn to fetch his hat and coat, Simmonds turned to Barnaby and held out his hand. "Congratulations, Mr. Adair. You're the father of a healthy boy with a very sound set of lungs. Mrs. Adair is also well. She sent a message for you—that you could stop worrying now."

"Oh." Barnaby stood stock still, taking it all in—or trying to. He had a son. And Penelope was clearly well—indeed, in her usual, crisply bossy state.

With an understanding smile, Simmonds turned to bow to the earl. "My lord."

Then Mostyn, also beaming, was there with Simmonds's coat and hat. Shrugging on the former, Simmonds glanced at Barnaby. "The ladies said you could go up now—no need to wait any longer."

Instantly, Barnaby refocused. "Thank you." With barely a nod, he went up the stairs, taking the steps three at a time.

His mother was waiting at the door, her eyes misty, her face wreathed in smiles. "Come in, come in. You have the most perfectly beautiful son."

He'd expected some degree of chaos. Instead, the room was tidy, serene, with no sign of the bowls and towels and what-not he was sure must have been there. Everything had been cleared, and a sense of joyous peace pervaded…then again, given the caliber of the ladies Penelope had had attending her, he really shouldn't have been surprised.

But from the moment his eyes lighted on the figure—the two of them —in the big bed, he saw no one and nothing else.

He wasn't even aware of crossing the room, but he must have; he found himself staring down in wonder at Penelope, her dark head bent as she lightly traced the curve of the tiny shell-like ear of the baby in her arms.

She glanced up, and although her eyes were weary and her face was pale, her smile was gloriously radiant; it lit his heart. "Here he is. And I have to say he really is quite fascinating. Did you hear him yell?"

For the first time in hours, Barnaby's lips curved. "The whole house heard. Simmonds said he has a good set of lungs."

Penelope grinned, but her expression instantly reverted to a glowing smile the like of which Barnaby hadn't seen before as she looked back at their son. Her attitude—full of open wonderment—said she was as delighted and intrigued, as rapt in this new little person as Barnaby was.

Gently letting himself down on the bed beside her, he joined her in staring, in marveling.

Putting out a tentative finger, he stroked the baby's hand. The tiny hand moved, then the even tinier fingers flexed, stretched, then closed and curled about Barnaby's single digit. His heart constricted. After a moment, he murmured, "He's perfect."

Penelope shot him one of her looks. "Of course, he is." But she was smiling.

The other ladies moved about the room, quietly organizing.

Then Penelope glanced at Barnaby. "Here—you should hold him."

Panic threatened, but, surrounded by all the females of her family, he girded his loins and somewhat gingerly accepted the bundle Penelope eased into his arms.

"Like this." She tugged his hand into position so that he was supporting the baby's head.

Gently cradling his son against his chest, Barnaby felt emotion well. It wasn't simply the reality of the lightly swaddled weight, but the tension in the shifting, tentatively squirming limbs that brought home that this wasn't a doll but a live little human. One who would grow, who through the next years would depend on Barnaby and Penelope to care for him, to see to his needs and his safety.

Joy, responsibility, and commitment—all rushed through Barnaby in that moment.

He glanced at Penelope; she met his gaze and he saw the same realization in her eyes.

This small person was theirs to care for, and he would be a constant in their lives from now on.

Minerva, Penelope's mother, touched Barnaby's shoulder. "Stand up, Barnaby, dear, and take him over there"—she waved to a clear space before the fireplace—"while we make Penelope more comfortable."

He did as he was bid and with his son in his arms retreated from the mayhem as the ladies descended in a flock upon the bed.

Standing before the fireplace, he looked into his son's face. He wondered what color his eyes would be—his bright blue or Penelope's dark brown? And what would his temperament be like? Like hers, or his, or somewhere between? How would they all get on? Would his son have the same comfortable relationship with his father as Barnaby had with the earl—a relationship built on understanding and shared interests?

How long he stood staring at his sleeping son's face and pondering the future he didn't know. About him, the ladies ebbed and flowed. His father came in briefly to be introduced to his latest grandson and to kiss Penelope's cheek, then the earl bore away Barnaby's mother after reminding her that she had a luncheon engagement that day, at which she would doubtless wish to share the news of the latest addition to her already large brood of grandchildren. The countess had duly kissed the baby's cheek, then kissed Barnaby's, and gone.

Shortly after, Emily, Anne, and Portia also took their leave. Penelope's mother, Minerva, would be remaining in Albemarle Street for the next week at least; after confirming that Penelope had all that she required, Minerva, too, came to kiss the baby's cheek, smile mistily at Barnaby before kissing his cheek, too, then, trailing her usual cloud of draperies, Minerva left them.

And, finally, there was just them—the three of them.

From across the room, Barnaby felt Penelope's gaze on his face, but for several minutes, she seemed content to simply watch him holding their son.

Eventually, however, she stirred. "So...who did it?"

Barnaby heard her, but her words made no sense. Lifting his head, he looked at her blankly, his mind floundering...he had no idea what she was asking about.

She stared at him, read his complete and utter befuddlement, and on a bubbling, laughing snort, she explained, "The case. Who killed Fletcher?"

"Ah." Barnaby blinked. The answer was there, the events of the past days clear enough in his mind, but it was as if they had occurred in a different age...they really weren't important anymore. As he turned his attention back to his son, he answered, "The butler did it."

EPILOGUE

*I*n the matter of the violent murder of Gordon Fletcher, Thomas Riggs was found guilty and hanged.

Lord Finsbury declined to bring charges against Katherine Mallard for her part in the temporary removal of the Finsbury diamonds from his safe. As the diamonds were back where they belonged, and the principal perpetrator of the scheme, namely Fletcher, had reaped a sentence far worse than any the law would have handed him, Stokes saw little benefit in further pursuing Kitty. Given her patently genuine attachment to Fletcher, Stokes doubted she would return to the game with any other man. Released from police custody, Kitty slipped away into London's teeming streets.

An announcement appeared in *The Times* in early January informing the world of the nuptials of Mr. Frederick Culver and Miss Gwendolyn Finsbury, only daughter of Godfrey, Lord Finsbury, and the late Maude Finsbury. The wedding was celebrated at the church in the village of Hampstead, which was noted as being the local church for both the Finsbury and the Culver families. The newly-weds had eschewed any travel in favor of settling into the large house Mr. Culver had inherited from his late parents.

Despite the formal wording, the announcement managed to convey a sense of deep and widely held satisfaction.

In the middle of January, as the culminating event of the lengthy Christmas and New Year family celebration the Countess of Cothelstone had insisted was her due, Oliver Lucas Barnaby Adair was christened in the chapel of Cothelstone Castle.

Later, as part of a much more private celebration, Barnaby presented Penelope with a black velvet case containing her very own diamond necklace, designed and executed to Barnaby's order by Aspreys of Bond Street.

"Oh! Oh! Oh!" Tugging the necklace from its case, Penelope literally leapt off the bed and dashed to the cheval mirror to don the heavy string and admire how it sat.

As she happened to be naked, Barnaby lay back on the pillows and enjoyed the display.

Penelope danced, turning this way and that, admiring the way the light fractured and sparkled in the heavy stones. "These are absolutely stunning!"

Swinging around, she raced back to the bed and all but flung herself on Barnaby.

Laughing, he caught her; holding her above him, he looked into her dark eyes. "Happy?"

Her face lit with the smile—that new smile that held such a deep contentment it never failed to strike to his heart. Holding his gaze, her hands on his shoulders, she replied, "I had no idea it was possible to *be* this happy."

As content as she, he let her roll to his side. She squinted down, fingering the bright stones. "Is it similar to the Finsbury necklace?"

"Yes and no. As per your instructions, I drew my inspiration from the Finsbury diamonds." Barnaby raised a hand and, with one finger, traced the links gracing her throat, then he met her eyes. "These, however, are better. These are real."

Penelope laughed and he laughed with her—then Oliver cried and she dashed to the crib and brought their son back to join them in the bed, and all was right—deeply, assuredly, and incontrovertibly right—in their world.

THE END

Dear Reader,

The Peculiar Case of Lord Finsbury's Diamonds was intended as a taste of what happened subsequent to the forming of the new relationships between Barnaby and Penelope, and Griselda and Stokes, as well as the two couples' commitment to investigating crime that grew out of the initial volume in THE CASEBOOK OF BARNABY ADAIR series, *Where the Heart Leads*. I hope you enjoyed reading about the evolution of those relationships.

And now my stage is set for the tales of Barnaby's investigations—THE CASEBOOK OF BARNABY ADAIR series—to roll forward. Three further books have already been published—in order they are: *The Masterful Mr. Montague, The Curious Case of Lady Latimer's Shoes,* and *Loving Rose: The Redemption of Malcolm Sinclair.* Two further novels are soon to be released—*The Confounding Case of the Carisbrook Emeralds* (June 14, 2018) and *The Murder at Mandeville Hall* (August 16, 2018). See below for further details.

Barnaby, Penelope, Stokes, Griselda, and their friends number among my favorite characters to write about. I hope they and their adventures solving mysteries and exposing villains entertain you as much as they do me.

Enjoy!

Stephanie.

For alerts as new books are released, plus information on upcoming books, exclusive sweepstakes and sneak peeks into upcoming novels, sign up for Stephanie's Private Email Newsletter
http://www.stephanielaurens.com/newsletter-signup/

The ultimate source for detailed information on all Stephanie's published books, including covers, descriptions, and excerpts, is Stephanie's Website www.stephanielaurens.com

You can also follow Stephanie via her Amazon Author Page at
http://tinyurl.com/zc3e9mp

Goodreads members can follow Stephanie via her author page
https://www.goodreads.com/author/show/9241.Stephanie_Laurens

You can email Stephanie at stephanie@stephanielaurens.com

Or find her on Facebook
https://www.facebook.com/AuthorStephanieLaurens/

COMING SOON IN THE CASEBOOK OF BARNABY ADAIR NOVELS:

The sixth volume in
The Casebook of Barnaby Adair mystery-romances
THE CONFOUNDING CASE OF THE CARISBROOK EMERALDS
To be released on June 14, 2018

#1 New York Times *bestselling author Stephanie Laurens brings you a tale of emerging and also established loves and the many facets of family, interwoven with mystery and murder.*

A young lady accused of theft and the gentleman who elects himself her champion enlist the aid of Stokes, Barnaby, Penelope, and friends in pursuing justice, only to find themselves tangled in a web of inter-family tensions and secrets.

When Miss Cara Di Abaccio is accused of stealing the Carisbrook emeralds by the infamously arrogant Lady Carisbrook and marched out of her guardian's house by Scotland Yard's finest, Hugo Adair, Barnaby Adair's cousin, takes umbrage and descends on Scotland Yard, breathing fire in Cara's defense.

Hugo discovers Inspector Stokes has been assigned to the case, and after surveying the evidence thus far, Stokes calls in his big guns when it comes to dealing with investigations in the ton—namely, the Honorable Barnaby Adair and his wife, Penelope.

Soon convinced of Cara's innocence and—given Hugo's apparent tendre for Cara—the need to clear her name, Penelope and Barnaby join

Stokes and his team in pursuing the emeralds and, most importantly, who stole them.

But the deeper our intrepid investigators delve into the Carisbrook household, the more certain they become that all is not as it seems. Lady Carisbrook is a harpy, Franklin Carisbrook is secretive, Julia Carisbrook is overly timid, and Lord Carisbrook, otherwise a genial and honorable gentleman, holds himself distant from his family. More, his lordship attempts to shut down the investigation. And Stokes, Barnaby, and Penelope are convinced the Carisbrooks' staff are not sharing all they know.

Meanwhile, having been appointed Cara's watchdog until the mystery is resolved, Hugo, fascinated by Cara as he's been with no other young lady, seeks to entertain and amuse her...and, increasingly intently, to discover the way to her heart. Consequently, Penelope finds herself juggling the attractions of the investigation against the demands of the Adair family for her to actively encourage the budding romance.

What would her mentors advise? On that, Penelope is crystal clear.

Regardless, aided by Griselda, Violet, and Montague and calling on contacts in business, the underworld, and ton society, Penelope, Barnaby, and Stokes battle to peel back each layer of subterfuge and, step by step, eliminate the innocent and follow the emeralds' trail...

Yet instead of becoming clearer, the veils and shadows shrouding the Carisbrooks only grow murkier...until, abruptly, our investigators find themselves facing an inexplicable death, with a potential murderer whose conviction would shake society to its back teeth.

A historical novel of 78,000 words interweaving mystery, romance, and social intrigue.

TO BE FOLLOWED BY:

The seventh volume in
The Casebook of Barnaby Adair mystery-romances
THE MURDER AT MANDEVILLE HALL
To be released on August 16, 2018

#1 New York Times *bestselling author Stephanie Laurens brings you a*

tale of unexpected romance that blossoms against the backdrop of dastardly murder.

On discovering the lifeless body of an innocent ingénue, a peer attending a country house party joins forces with the lady-amazon sent to fetch the victim safely home in a race to expose the murderer before Stokes, assisted by Barnaby and Penelope, is forced to allow the guests, murderer included, to decamp.

Well-born rakehell and head of an ancient family, Alaric, Lord Carradale, has finally acknowledged reality and is preparing to find a bride. But loyalty to his childhood friend, Percy Mandeville, necessitates attending Percy's annual house party, held at neighboring Mandeville Hall. Yet despite deploying his legendary languid charm, by the second evening of the week-long event, Alaric is bored and restless.

Escaping from the soirée and the Hall, Alaric decides that as soon as he's free, he'll hie to London and find the mild-mannered, biddable lady he believes will ensure a peaceful life. But the following morning, on walking through the Mandeville Hall shrubbery on his way to join the other guests, he comes upon the corpse of a young lady-guest.

Constance Whittaker accepts that no gentleman will ever offer for her —she's too old, too tall, too buxom, too headstrong...too much in myriad ways. Now acting as her grandfather's agent, she arrives at Mandeville Hall to extricate her young cousin, Glynis, who unwisely accepted an invitation to the reputedly licentious house party.

But Glynis cannot be found.

A search is instituted. Venturing into the shrubbery, Constance discovers an outrageously handsome aristocrat crouched beside Glynis's lifeless form. Unsurprisingly, Constance leaps to the obvious conclusion.

Luckily, once the gentleman explains that he'd only just arrived, commonsense reasserts itself. More, as matters unfold and she and Carradale have to battle to get Glynis's death properly investigated, Constance discovers Alaric to be a worthy ally.

Yet even after Inspector Stokes of Scotland Yard arrives and takes charge of the case, along with his consultants, the Honorable Barnaby Adair and his wife, Penelope, the murderer's identity remains shrouded in mystery, and learning why Glynis was killed—all in the few days before the house party's guests will insist on leaving—tests the resolve of all concerned. Flung into each other's company, fiercely independent though Constance is, unsusceptible though Alaric is, neither can deny the connection that grows between them.

Then Constance vanishes.

Can Alaric unearth the one fact that will point to the murderer before the villain rips from the world the lady Alaric now craves for his own?

A historical novel of 75,000 words interweaving romance, mystery, and murder.

ALSO SOON TO BE RELEASED:

The first volume in THE CAVANAUGHS
THE DESIGNS OF LORD RANDOLPH CAVANAUGH
To be released on April 24, 2018

#1 New York Times *bestselling author Stephanie Laurens returns with a new series that captures the simmering desires and intrigues of early Victorians as only she can. Ryder Cavanaugh's step-siblings are determined to make their own marks in London society. Seeking fortune and passion, THE CAVANAUGHS will delight readers with their bold exploits.*

An independent nobleman

Lord Randolph Cavanaugh is loyal and devoted—but only to family. To the rest of the world he's aloof and untouchable, a respected and driven entrepreneur. But Rand yearns for more in life, and when he travels to Buckinghamshire to review a recent investment, he discovers a passionate woman who will challenge his rigid self-control...

A determined lady

Felicia Throgmorton intends to keep her family afloat. For decades, her father was consumed by his inventions and now, months after his death, with their finances in ruins, her brother insists on continuing their father's tinkering. Felicia is desperate to hold together what's left of the estate. Then she discovers she must help persuade their latest investor that her father's follies are a risk worth taking...

Together—the perfect team

Rand arrives at Throgmorton Hall to discover the invention on which he's staked his reputation has exploded, the inventor is not who he expected, and a fiercely intelligent woman now holds the key to his future success. But unflinching courage in the face of dismaying hurdles is a trait they share, and Rand and Felicia are forced to act together against ruthless foes to protect everything they hold dear.

RECENTLY RELEASED:

The first volume in Lady Osbaldestone's Christmas Chronicles
LADY OSBALDESTONE'S CHRISTMAS GOOSE

#1 New York Times *bestselling author Stephanie Laurens brings you a lighthearted tale of Christmas long ago with a grandmother and three of her grandchildren, one lost soul, a lady driven to distraction, a recalcitrant donkey, and a flock of determined geese.*

Three years after being widowed, Therese, Lady Osbaldestone finally settles into her dower property of Hartington Manor in the village of Little Moseley in Hampshire. She is in two minds as to whether life in the small village will generate sufficient interest to keep her amused over the months when she is not in London or visiting friends around the country. But she will see.

It's December, 1810, and Therese is looking forward to her usual Christmas with her family at Winslow Abbey, her youngest daughter, Celia's home. But then a carriage rolls up and disgorges Celia's three oldest children. Their father has contracted mumps, and their mother has sent the three—Jamie, George, and Lottie—to spend this Christmas with their grandmama in Little Moseley.

Therese has never had to manage small children, not even her own. She assumes the children will keep themselves amused, but quickly learns that what amuses three inquisitive, curious, and confident youngsters isn't compatible with village peace. Just when it seems she will have to set her mind to inventing something, she and the children learn that with only twelve days to go before Christmas, the village flock of geese has vanished.

Every household in the village is now missing the centerpiece of their Christmas feast. But how could an entire flock go missing without the slightest trace? The children are as mystified and as curious as Therese—

and she seizes on the mystery as the perfect distraction for the three children as well as herself.

But while searching for the geese, she and her three helpers stumble on two locals who, it is clear, are in dire need of assistance in sorting out their lives. Never one to shy from a little matchmaking, Therese undertakes to guide Miss Eugenia Fitzgibbon into the arms of the determinedly reclusive Lord Longfellow. To her considerable surprise, she discovers that her grandchildren have inherited skills and talents from both her late husband as well as herself. And with all the customary village events held in the lead up to Christmas, she and her three helpers have opportunities galore in which to subtly nudge and steer.

Yet while their matchmaking appears to be succeeding, neither they nor anyone else have found so much as a feather from the village's geese. Larceny is ruled out; a flock of that size could not have been taken from the area without someone noticing. So where could the birds be? And with the days passing and Christmas inexorably approaching, will they find the blasted birds in time?

First in series. A novel of 60,000 words. A Christmas tale of romance and geese.

AND FOR HOW IT ALL BEGAN...

Read about Penelope's and Barnaby's romance, plus that of Stokes and Griselda, in
The first volume in
The Casebook of Barnaby Adair mystery-romances
WHERE THE HEART LEADS

Penelope Ashford, Portia Cynster's younger sister, has grown up with every advantage - wealth, position, and beauty. Yet Penelope is anything but a typical ton miss - forceful, willful and blunt to a fault, she has for years devoted her considerable energy and intelligence to directing an institution caring for the forgotten orphans of London's streets.

But now her charges are mysteriously disappearing. Desperate, Penelope turns to the one man she knows who might help her - Barnaby Adair.

Handsome scion of a noble house, Adair has made a name for

himself in political and judicial circles. His powers of deduction and observation combined with his pedigree has seen him solve several serious crimes within the ton. Although he makes her irritatingly uncomfortable, Penelope throws caution to the wind and appears on his bachelor doorstep late one night, determined to recruit him to her cause.

Barnaby is intrigued—by her story, and her. Her bold beauty and undeniable brains make a striking contrast to the usual insipid ton misses. And as he's in dire need of an excuse to avoid said insipid misses, he accepts her challenge, never dreaming she and it will consume his every waking hour.

Enlisting the aid of Inspector Basil Stokes of the fledgling Scotland Yard, they infiltrate the streets of London's notorious East End. But as they unravel the mystery of the missing boys, they cross the trail of a criminal embedded in the very organization recently created to protect all Londoners. And that criminal knows of them and their efforts, and is only too ready to threaten all they hold dear, including their new-found knowledge of the intrigues of the human heart.

FURTHER CASES AND THE EVOLUTION OF RELATIONSHIPS CONTINUE IN:

The third volume in
The Casebook of Barnaby Adair mystery-romances
THE MASTERFUL MR. MONTAGUE

Montague has devoted his life to managing the wealth of London's elite, but at a huge cost: a family of his own. Then the enticing Miss Violet Matcham seeks his help, and in the puzzle she presents him, he finds an intriguing new challenge professionally...and personally.

Violet, devoted lady-companion to the aging Lady Halstead, turns to Montague to reassure her ladyship that her affairs are in order. But the famous Montague is not at all what she'd expected—this man is compelling, decisive, supportive, and strong—everything Violet needs in a champion, a position to which Montague rapidly lays claim.

But then Lady Halstead is murdered and Violet and Montague, aided by Barnaby Adair, Inspector Stokes, Penelope, and Griselda, race to expose a cunning and cold-blooded killer...who stalks closer and closer.

Will Montague and Violet learn the shocking truth too late to seize their chance at enduring love?

A pre-Victorian tale of romance and mystery in the classic historical romance style. A novel of 120,000 words.

The fourth volume in
The Casebook of Barnaby Adair mystery-romances
THE CURIOUS CASE OF LADY LATIMER'S SHOES

#1 New York Times *bestselling author Stephanie Laurens brings you a tale of mysterious death, feuding families, star-crossed lovers—and shoes to die for.*

With her husband, amateur-sleuth the Honorable Barnaby Adair, decidedly eccentric fashionable matron Penelope Adair is attending the premier event opening the haut ton's Season when a body is discovered in the gardens. A lady has been struck down with a finial from the terrace balustrade. Her family is present, as are the cream of the haut ton—the shocked hosts turn to Barnaby and Penelope for help.

Barnaby calls in Inspector Basil Stokes and they begin their investigation. Penelope assists by learning all she can about the victim's family, and uncovers a feud between them and the Latimers over the fabulous shoes known as Lady Latimer's shoes, currently exclusive to the Latimers.

The deeper Penelope delves, the more convinced she becomes that the murder is somehow connected to the shoes. She conscripts Griselda, Stokes's wife, and Violet Montague, now Penelope's secretary, and the trio set out to learn all they can about the people involved and most importantly the shoes, a direction vindicated when unexpected witnesses report seeing a lady fleeing the scene—wearing Lady Latimer's shoes.

But nothing is as it seems, and the more Penelope and her friends learn about the shoes, conundrums abound, compounded by a Romeo-and-Juliet romance and escalating social pressure...until at last the pieces fall into place, and finally understanding what has occurred, the six intrepid investigators race to prevent an even worse tragedy.

A pre-Victorian mystery with strong elements of romance. A novel of 76,000 words.

The fifth volume in
The Casebook of Barnaby Adair mystery-romances
LOVING ROSE: THE REDEMPTION OF MALCOLM SINCLAIR

#1 New York Times *bestselling author Stephanie Laurens returns with another thrilling story from the Casebook of Barnaby Adair...*

Miraculously spared from death, Malcolm Sinclair erases the notorious man he once was. Reinventing himself as Thomas Glendower, he strives to make amends for his past, yet he never imagines penance might come via a secretive lady he discovers living in his secluded manor.

Rose has a plausible explanation for why she and her children are residing in Thomas's house, but she quickly realizes he's far too intelligent to fool. Revealing the truth is impossibly dangerous, yet day by day, he wins her trust, and then her heart.

But then her enemy closes in, and Rose turns to Thomas as the only man who can protect her and the children. And when she asks for his help, Thomas finally understands his true purpose, and with unwavering commitment, he seeks his redemption in the only way he can—through living the reality of loving Rose.

A pre-Victorian tale of romance and mystery in the classic historical romance style. A novel of 105,000 words.

ABOUT THE AUTHOR

#1 *New York Times* bestselling author Stephanie Laurens began writing romances as an escape from the dry world of professional science. Her hobby quickly became a career when her first novel was accepted for publication, and with entirely becoming alacrity, she gave up writing about facts in favor of writing fiction.

All Laurens's works to date are historical romances ranging from medieval times to the mid-1800s, and her settings range from Scotland to India. The majority of her works are set in the period of the British Regency. Laurens has published more than 70 works of historical romance, including 39 *New York Times* bestsellers and has sold more than 20 million print, audio, and e-books globally. All her works are continuously available in print and e-book formats in English worldwide, and have been translated into many other languages. An international bestseller, among other accolades, Laurens has received the Romance Writers of America® prestigious RITA® Award for Best Romance Novella 2008 for *The Fall of Rogue Gerrard.*

Laurens's continuing novels featuring the Cynster family are widely regarded as classics of the historical romance genre. Other series include the *Bastion Club Novels*, the *Black Cobra Quartet*, the *Adventurers Quartet*, and the *Casebook of Barnaby Adair Novels.*

For information on all published novels and on upcoming releases and updates on novels yet to come, visit Stephanie's website: www.stephanielaurens.com

To sign up for Stephanie's Email Newsletter (a private list) for heads-up alerts as new books are released, exclusive sneak peeks into upcoming books, and exclusive sweepstakes contests, follow the prompts on Stephanie's Email Newsletter Sign-up Page on her website.

Stephanie lives with her husband and a goofy black labradoodle in the hills outside Melbourne, Australia. When she isn't writing, she's reading, and if she isn't reading, she'll be tending her garden.

CPSIA information can be obtained
at www.ICGtesting.com
Printed in the USA
LVOW13s1735130718
583538LV00013BA/1094/P